Savage Tides

SURVIVAL AND DESIRE

JULIE FREEBUSH

SFD PUBLICATIONS

Contents

CHAPTER ONE

Golden Handcuffs

The Cartier diamond necklace lay cool against Eliza Harrington's skin, a delicious contrast to the heat of hundreds of eyes tracking her every move. The annual Oceanside Conservation Gala was Manhattan's premier charity event, and Eliza knew her entrance had been perfect—the custom Valentino gown clinging to her curves before cascading to the floor in a waterfall of midnight blue silk, her honey-blonde hair swept up to showcase both the jewels and the elegant column of her neck.

"There she is," Richard's voice carried that particular note of pride he reserved for introducing his prized acquisitions—whether companies or wives. "The woman who makes all this worthwhile."

Eliza activated her practiced smile, the one that revealed just enough of her perfect teeth while softening her eyes to suggest both warmth and mystery. Five years of marriage to one of New York's most successful hedge fund managers had perfected her timing.

"This is my wife, Eliza," Richard continued, his hand possessively circling her waist, fingers pressing against her hip bone. "Eliza, meet Harrison Blackwell and James Morrison from Apex Capital."

"Enchanted," she murmured, extending her hand with precisely the right angle of her wrist. The older of the two men, Harrison, held her fingers a moment too long.

"Richard never mentioned his wife was so stunning," Harrison said, eyes lingering on the plunging neckline of her gown.

"Didn't he?" Eliza laughed lightly, the sound practiced to perfection. "How terribly unlike him. It's usually the first thing he tells people."

As Richard launched into discussions about market forecasts and potential investments, Eliza maintained her position, her body language attentive while her mind wandered. She'd performed this dance countless times—the smiling, supportive wife who understood her role was to enhance Richard's image while knowing when to fade into ornamental silence.

Three more hours, she calculated. *Then I can get out of these shoes.*

Across the ballroom, Eliza caught the gaze of a younger woman—perhaps twenty-five—in a simple black dress. Something in the woman's expression sliced through Eliza's practiced poise. Not envy or admiration, but something worse—pity. As if she saw past the diamonds and designer labels to something Eliza herself tried never to acknowledge.

Eliza broke the connection first, turning to touch Richard's arm. "Darling, I'm going to find Charlotte. You gentlemen enjoy your discussion."

As she glided away, champagne flute in hand, Eliza pushed aside the momentary discomfort. What did that girl know about anything? At thirty-two, Eliza had secured what most women spent their lives chasing—financial security, social position, and a lifestyle of uncompromised luxury.

Yet as she air-kissed her way through the crowd, the young woman's look lingered in her mind like a discordant note in an otherwise perfect symphony.

The Carrara marble bathroom in their Central Park West penthouse gleamed in the morning light as Eliza methodically worked through her beauty regimen. The night before felt distant now, replaced by the comforting ritual of self-maintenance.

She studied her reflection with clinical detachment—assessing rather than admiring. At thirty-two, she still received the hunger in men's eyes that had first caught Richard's attention when she was twenty-seven. Her skin remained firm, her body toned through disciplined exercise and careful nutrition. Beauty was currency, and Eliza was meticulous about protecting her investments.

She applied the $600 serum with gentle upward strokes, counting silently. Twenty-five on each side. The bathroom door opened behind her, Richard's reflection appearing in the mirror. At fifty-two, he remained handsome in that distinguished silver-fox way—his hair more salt than pepper now, but his physique maintained by regular sessions with an expensive personal trainer.

"Morning," he mumbled, barely glancing at her as he reached for his electric toothbrush. "How was the rest of the gala? I lost track of you."

"Lovely," Eliza replied automatically. "Charlotte mentioned they've booked Mauritius for Christmas. Apparently, Bali is passé now."

Richard rinsed and spat. "Sounds expensive. Michael must be doing well."

"Or Charlotte is," Eliza countered with a smile that didn't reach her eyes.

They moved around each other with practiced efficiency—two performers in a choreographed routine that required little thought. Richard checking his stock portfolios while Eliza applied her makeup; his shower timed perfectly to conclude as she finished her hair; his tie selection presented for her approval without either of them acknowledging the ritual.

When the envelope arrived with the morning mail, Eliza recognized the Amex Centurion statement immediately. She slit it open while Richard spoke to his assistant on the phone, scrolling through the six-figure balance with practiced indifference. The Bergdorf shopping spree, the spa weekend in Connecticut, the impulse purchase of that limited-edition handbag—all of it adding up to more than most people earned in years.

She felt Richard's eyes on her as she set the statement aside.

"Damaging month?" he asked, a hint of amusement in his voice.

"No more than usual," she replied with practiced lightness.

"Good." He nodded once, turning back to his call. The freedom to spend was part of their unspoken agreement. Her beauty and social grace for his financial support—a transaction they both understood without acknowledging.

Eliza watched him leave the bathroom, the expensive fabric of his suit molding to his still-trim physique. She'd chosen that suit, as she chose most things in their shared life. Her taste was impeccable—one of the qualities Richard valued most.

Turning back to the mirror, she finished applying her lipstick with a steady hand, the cool berry shade complementing her complexion perfectly. The woman staring back was flawless, polished, desirable.

Why, then, did the bathroom suddenly feel so cold?

"You're practically glowing, Eliza! What's your secret?" Charlotte Westfield leaned forward over their salads at Le Bernardin, her surgically enhanced features arranged in an expression of conspiracy.

"Clean living," Eliza replied with a laugh, knowing the response would amuse her lunch companions.

The table of five women—all married to men in Richard's circle—tittered appreciatively. These monthly lunches were part performance, part intelligence gathering, and occasionally, rarely, moments of genuine connection.

"If by clean you mean that new facial Svetlana is offering at Rejuvenate, I'm right there with you," said Pamela, whose husband ran a technology investment firm. "Two thousand dollars for someone to essentially sandblast your face, but damn if it doesn't work."

The conversation flowed around Eliza as she sipped her Sancerre, contributing just enough to maintain her position while observing the subtle competitions playing out. Veronica casually mentioning the private jet her husband had recently upgraded. Charlotte describing their new summer home in the Hamptons, carefully establishing it was in a better location than Pamela's.

"I heard Richard closed that massive deal with the Singapore group," Veronica said suddenly, turning to Eliza. "That must be what—his third major acquisition this quarter?"

Eliza smiled, recognizing the probe for information. "Richard doesn't bore me with the details. But yes, I believe it went well."

She'd learned early in their marriage that appearing somewhat detached from Richard's business enhanced her mystique among these women. Let them wonder if she was too secure to care or too frivolous to understand. Either served her purpose.

The waiter appeared with their second round of drinks, and as the conversation shifted to a scandal involving another hedge fund wife, Eliza's mind drifted back to her life before Richard. The cramped apartment shared with three other aspiring models. The calculation of whether to buy groceries or pay for portfolio shots. The casting directors with wandering hands and empty promises.

She'd been twenty-seven when Richard spotted her at a gallery opening—there as eye candy for a photographer who'd promised exposure to wealthy patrons. Richard had bypassed the photographer entirely, approaching her directly with a confidence born of never being denied what he wanted.

"Do you actually like any of the art?" he'd asked, startling her with a question that assumed she had opinions.

Their courtship had been swift and overwhelmingly lavish. Richard had pursued her with the same strategic focus he applied to acquisitions, and Eliza had recognized the opportunity for what it was—her best chance at the security that had eluded her since childhood.

"...wouldn't you agree, Eliza?" Charlotte's voice pulled her back to the present.

"I'm sorry, I was elsewhere for a moment," Eliza admitted.

"I was saying," Charlotte repeated with a smirk, "that our husbands may provide the lifestyle, but we earn our keep in other ways."

The table erupted in knowing laughter, and Eliza joined in, though something about the phrasing—*earn our keep*—landed uncomfortably. It was too close to acknowledging what they all pretended didn't exist: the transactional nature underlying their marriages.

"Speaking of earning our keep," Veronica lowered her voice conspiratorially, "Mitchell was completely useless last night. Three minutes, done, snoring. I swear, sometimes I wonder why I bother with the La Perla."

The women launched into stories of sexual disappointment and strategies for minimizing effort while maximizing results. Eliza contributed her own carefully edited anecdote, revealing enough to participate without exposing anything genuine.

As dessert arrived—shared plates to maintain the illusion of indulgence without its consequences—Eliza found herself wondering if any of these women experienced real desire for their husbands, or if they all performed the same calculated seductions she did.

And why that question suddenly mattered when it never had before.

Richard's key in the door awakened Eliza from her light doze on the living room chaise. The clock on the wall showed 10:37 PM—earlier than she'd expected him. She quickly smoothed her silk negligee and arranged herself in what experience had shown was his preferred position—one leg slightly extended, hair cascading over one shoulder.

"You're home," she called softly, pitching her voice to carry just enough warmth.

Richard appeared in the doorway, his tie already loosened, the faint scent of scotch accompanying him. His gaze swept over her, acknowledgment rather than appreciation in his eyes.

"The Prescott deal is finally closed," he said, setting his briefcase down and rolling his shoulders. "Eight months of negotiations, but we got them at the price point we wanted."

Eliza rose gracefully, moving toward him with practiced sensuality. "That's wonderful, darling. You must be exhausted." She reached to help him out of his jacket, her fingers brushing his shoulders with deliberate lightness. "Let me help you unwind."

Richard allowed her ministrations, his mind clearly still in the boardroom. Eliza persisted, knowing the vacation she wanted hinged on catching him in a satisfied mood. She'd received the yacht broker's portfolio that morning—a luxury charter through the Caribbean islands, perfectly timed for their anniversary.

"I've been thinking about our anniversary," she murmured, unbuttoning his shirt with expert precision. "Five years deserves something special."

"Hmm?" Richard focused on her more fully now, though his interest seemed more habitual than passionate. "Did you have something in mind? Another piece from Van Cleef?"

"Actually," Eliza let her lips brush his ear as she removed his cufflinks, "I was thinking of an experience rather than a thing. Something memorable."

She guided him toward the bedroom, continuing her gentle seduction. By the time she'd outlined the yacht charter—emphasizing the exclusivity of the route and the broker's mention that a rival hedge fund manager had been interested but couldn't secure the dates—Richard was reclining against their pillows, his interest finally engaged.

"Salvatore mentioned it?" he asked, referring to his most direct competitor. "And he couldn't get the booking?"

"Apparently not," Eliza confirmed, straddling him with practiced ease. "The broker mentioned it would be featured in Robb Report next season."

Richard's hands found her hips, his grip tightening as he considered the prestige. "Could be worth looking into."

Eliza smiled, recognizing victory even before it was fully secured. She bent to kiss him, performing the sequence of movements she knew would bring him fastest to completion. Richard responded with mechanical enthusiasm, his hands moving along her body in familiar patterns.

Their lovemaking followed its usual choreography—effi-cient, mutually considerate in a technical sense, and utterly de-void of surprise. Eliza made the sounds she knew he expected, moved the way experience had taught her he preferred, and brought them both to a conclusion that satisfied the physical urge without touching anything deeper.

Afterward, Richard fell almost immediately into sleep, while Eliza lay awake beside him. The yacht charter was as good as secured now; she'd succeeded in her night's objective. Yet as she listened to his even breathing, she found herself wondering about the woman at the gala and her pitying look.

What would you know about it? Eliza thought defensively. *You couldn't possibly understand the trade-offs, the calculations.*

But in the darkness of their penthouse bedroom, surround-ed by the trappings of the life she'd so carefully secured, Eliza admitted to herself what she never would to others: the young woman had recognized something true. That beneath the de-signer gowns and diamond jewelry, despite the enviable Insta-gram posts and society page mentions, Eliza Harrington was a woman in golden handcuffs—adorned and imprisoned by the same gleaming bonds.

She turned away from her sleeping husband, curling into herself as if for protection.

It doesn't matter, she told herself firmly. *This is the life I chose. This is the life I want.*

The silence of the bedroom offered no contradiction, but neither did it offer confirmation.

CHAPTER TWO

Anniversary Plans

Sunlight spilled through the floor-to-ceiling windows of the Harringtons' breakfast nook, warming Eliza's bare shoulders as she sipped her green tea. The New York skyline stretched before her—a vista that had once thrilled her but now barely registered. She scrolled idly through her Instagram feed, pausing occasionally to like photos posted by women in her social circle, each carefully curated image more flawless than the last.

The sound of Richard's footsteps pulled her attention away from the screen. His smile—that rare, genuine expression—immediately put her on alert. Richard's unscheduled displays of happiness usually meant a major business coup or an extravagant purchase.

"I have something for you," he announced, placing a leather portfolio on the table beside her tea.

Eliza raised an eyebrow, setting her phone aside. "It's not our anniversary for another two weeks."

"Consider this the preamble." Richard sat across from her, watching with evident satisfaction as she untied the leather cord.

Inside, Eliza found glossy brochures featuring a sleek, 150-foot yacht gleaming against turquoise waters. Her breath caught—it was exactly what she'd suggested during their intimate moment, but far more luxurious than she'd expected.

"Is this—"

"The Aurora," Richard confirmed. "Seventy-two thousand per week, crew of twelve, five staterooms. I've secured it for three weeks, starting on our anniversary."

Genuine excitement rippled through Eliza. Despite the calculated nature of their relationship, there were still moments when Richard managed to surprise her. She flipped through the brochures, fingertips tracing over images of sun-drenched decks, elegant dining areas, and sumptuous bedrooms.

"Richard, it's perfect." Her smile wasn't performed this time.

He nodded, clearly pleased with her reaction. "The route is exclusive—some of the most remote islands in the Caribbean. Places regular tourists never see."

"Three weeks?" Eliza leaned forward. "You'll be away from the office that long?"

Richard's expression shifted subtly, business calculation replacing momentary warmth. "Not entirely. The yacht has satellite communications, and I've invited James Morrison and his wife for the middle week. The Morrison deal needs nurturing."

Of course. Eliza kept her smile in place despite the slight deflation of her excitement. The trip wasn't just for them—it was another business opportunity, another stage for their performance.

"Which islands?" she asked, redirecting the conversation.

As Richard detailed their itinerary, Eliza found herself imagining the photographs she'd capture—her tanned body against pristine sands, cocktail in hand as she lounged on the yacht's deck, sunset silhouetting her figure in some sheer resort dress. The mental images she composed had nothing to do with experiencing paradise and everything to do with showcasing it.

"Salvatore attempted to book the same yacht," Richard added with poorly concealed satisfaction. "Apparently, they couldn't accommodate his dates."

"How unfortunate for him," Eliza murmured, recognizing the true source of Richard's pleasure. The yacht wasn't just transportation; it was a victory lap.

She returned to the brochures, genuinely appreciating the luxury they promised while simultaneously calculating the social capital each location would provide. The untouched beaches would serve as perfect backdrops for the carefully casual photos that would make her followers seethe with envy.

"Thank you," she said, reaching across to squeeze Richard's hand. "It's the perfect anniversary gift."

Richard nodded, his attention already shifting to his watch. "I need to head in. Early meeting with Tokyo."

As he stood to leave, Eliza remained at the table, surrounded by images of paradise while mentally categorizing which designers she would need to shop for appropriate attire. The trip would be another performance, but at least the stage would be spectacular.

———◄O►———

"Perhaps the cerulean? The color brings out your eyes."

Eliza considered her reflection in the mirror as the Neiman Marcus personal shopper held up a shimmering silk cover-up. The color was stunning against her honey-toned skin, the fabric so lightweight it seemed to float around her body.

"Yes," she agreed. "And the white one as well."

The young woman—Sophia, according to her discreet name tag—beamed with the satisfaction of a successful suggestion. "Excellent choices, Mrs. Harrington. Shall we look at evening wear next? I've pulled several pieces I think would be perfect for sunset cocktails on a yacht."

For the past three hours, Eliza had been the center of an elaborate retail ritual. When you regularly dropped five figures in a single shopping trip, stores ensured your experience was nothing short of reverent. A private suite had been prepared, champagne was flowing, and a team of associates hovered attentively, anticipating her every need.

"Let's finish swimwear first," Eliza directed, turning to examine her profile in the mirror.

She wore a barely-there bikini in pale gold, the fabric clinging to her curves like a second skin. At thirty-two, her body remained enviable—the result of punishing workout regimens and dietary discipline. Still, she scrutinized herself with merciless eyes, noting the almost imperceptible softening at her hip, the faint lines beginning to form around her eyes when she smiled.

Sophia approached with another swimsuit—a one-piece this time, with strategic cutouts that would reveal just enough skin to be enticing while concealing the minor imperfections Eliza perceived.

"Brazilian cut in the back," Sophia noted. "Very on-trend this season."

Eliza nodded, running her fingertips over the luxurious fabric. These weren't just garments; they were armor, carefully selected to enhance her value in the economy of beauty and status. Each piece needed to photograph perfectly while suggesting accessibility—the illusion that paradise was attainable rather than purchased at extraordinary cost.

"I'll try it," she decided.

As Sophia helped her into the new suit, Eliza caught herself wondering what the sales associate really thought of her. Did she envy Eliza's wealth and beauty, or did she see through to the calculation beneath? The thought was uncomfortable, reminiscent of the pitying look from the woman at the gala.

"Stunning," Sophia breathed when the suit was in place.

Eliza studied her reflection, turning to see how the fabric accentuated her curves. The suit would photograph beautifully against white sand beaches. She could already envision the caption: *Just another day in paradise* #blessed #islandlife.

"I'll take this one too," she decided.

The shopping continued with the precision of a military campaign. Resort dresses, evening gowns, day wear, accessories—all selected with meticulous attention to color palettes that would complement the Caribbean setting.

On a whim, Eliza ventured into the store's newly installed "Adventure Outfitters" section, where luxury brands had begun catering to wealthy clients' growing interest in stylish survivalism.

"We just received this collection," an eager associate informed her, presenting what appeared to be a designer interpretation of hiking boots—all buttery leather and unnecessary gold hardware.

"For island exploration," Eliza mused, though she had no real intention of venturing beyond manicured beaches.

She selected the boots, a ridiculously overpriced "survival kit" housed in a Louis Vuitton case, and a compass pendant that was more jewelry than functional tool. Each item was a fashion statement disguised as practical gear, its true utility limited to the carefully curated image of adventurous leisure it would project.

In the fitting room, Eliza slipped into a sheer linen dress, the fabric caressing her skin with sensuous lightness. She imagined wearing it on the yacht's deck, the setting sun turning the white fabric translucent, outlining her silhouette for Richard's appreciative gaze—or perhaps for the crew's surreptitious glances.

The thought caught her by surprise. Why would she care about the crew's attention?

"Mrs. Harrington?" Sophia's voice interrupted her thoughts. "Would you like to see the sandals we discussed?"

"Yes," Eliza replied, shaking off the momentary distraction. "And I'll need at least three more swimsuits."

By the time the shopping expedition concluded, Eliza had spent enough to fund a modest home purchase. The associates beamed as they arranged delivery of her selections to the penthouse, their commission-fueled smiles as practiced as her own social expressions.

As her driver helped her into the car, Eliza felt the peculiar emptiness that often followed these indulgences—a hollowness that no amount of cashmere or silk seemed able to fill.

"The beauty of the Aurora," Richard was saying, "is the exclusivity. The yacht only books ten charters per year. Most of the time, it's reserved for the owner's personal use."

Eliza maintained her attentive expression as her husband detailed the vessel's specifications to the dinner party for what felt like the hundredth time. The private dining room at Eleven Madison Park hummed with the murmured conversations of New York's financial elite, the lighting carefully designed to flatter aging complexions.

James Morrison nodded appreciatively, his wife Katherine reaching for her wine glass with a tight smile. "Sounds spectacular. What's the crew like?"

"First-rate," Richard assured him. "Captain has twenty years of experience, former luxury cruise liner officer. The chef trained under Thomas Keller."

Eliza let her gaze drift around the table. Three couples besides herself and Richard—all connected to the Morrison deal in some capacity. The men in nearly identical suits, the women varying only in the designers they wore and the colors they'd chosen. A tableau of wealth so uniform it approached parody.

"Eliza selected the itinerary," Richard added, surprising her with the attribution. "She has quite the eye for these things."

Instantly, all attention shifted to her. Eliza smoothly filled the expectant pause.

"We'll be exploring some of the more remote islands," she explained, leaning forward just enough to create a subtle display of décolletage. "Places where the beaches remain pristine and the local culture hasn't been overtaken by tourism."

She had no idea if this was true—she'd merely approved the broker's suggested route—but the description painted the appropriate picture of exclusive access.

"I can't wait to see it," Katherine Morrison replied with a hint of envy.

"You're going to love it Kat," Eliza offered, knowing Richard had invited them for a week in an effort to close yet another big deal. "We can sip cocktails and soak up the sun laying on a private beach, while these two plan their takeover of Wall Street."

Richard's hand found her knee beneath the table, a subtle signal of approval. Eliza had performed her role perfectly, the perfect wingman that would facilitate his further business discussions in a relaxed setting.

As the men returned to discussing market forecasts, Eliza felt Paul Westfield's gaze lingering on her from across the table. Charlotte's husband had always been obvious in his appreciation of Eliza's beauty, his eyes frequently dropping to her neckline or lingering on her legs when Charlotte wasn't watching.

Normally, Eliza ignored such attention—it was simply part of the background radiation of being an attractive woman in these circles. Tonight, however, she found herself subtly responding, angling her body to better display her figure, maintaining eye contact a moment longer than necessary when he addressed her.

The small rebellion gave her an unexpected thrill. Not because she had any interest in Paul—he was as bland and entitled as most of Richard's associates—but because it was unscripted, a departure from her carefully managed role.

"I understand the crew includes some interesting characters," Charles Davis commented, interrupting her thoughts. "Former naval officers, competitive sailors. A step above the usual staff."

Richard nodded. "Absolutely. The deckhand—Marco, I believe—was some kind of survival expert. Military background. The broker mentioned it as a security feature."

Something about the mention of this unknown crew member stirred Eliza's curiosity. A survival expert on a luxury yacht seemed incongruous, like her own purchases of designer "exploration" boots.

"How reassuring," she murmured, her tone deliberately provocative. "A man who knows how to handle himself in difficult situations."

She felt Richard's glance, sensed his momentary confusion at her uncharacteristic comment. Eliza maintained her composed smile, even as she wondered at her own impulse to disrupt the evening's carefully orchestrated flow.

As dinner progressed, Eliza found herself increasingly performing the role of desirable accessory, allowing her gaze to linger on each man just long enough to make him feel special while never crossing the line into impropriety. It was a dance she'd perfected—the enhancement of Richard's status through the implication that he possessed what other men desired.

Richard basked in the reflected glory, his hand occasionally claiming her waist or shoulder in subtle displays of ownership that the other men recognized and envied. By dessert, the

Morrison deal seemed all but secured, facilitated by the social lubrication Eliza had provided.

"To new ventures," Richard proposed as espresso was served, raising his glass in a toast that carried multiple meanings.

Glasses clinked, and Eliza caught Paul watching her lips as she sipped her wine. The game was trivial but provided momentary diversion from the emptiness that increasingly haunted her perfect life.

Later, as they drove home, his satisfaction was palpable.

"You were perfect tonight," he told her, his hand resting possessively on her thigh. "Morrison is completely on board now. I suspect having them on the yacht for a few days will seal the deal."

"I'm glad," Eliza replied, staring out at the city lights.

Richard squeezed her leg, his hand sliding higher. "You looked stunning in that dress. Did you notice how Paul couldn't keep his eyes off you?"

So he had noticed. Eliza turned to him, intrigued by his reaction. "Does that bother you?"

"Quite the opposite," Richard admitted, his voice lowering. "It's gratifying to have what other men want."

The honesty of his response should have been offensive, but Eliza found it refreshingly direct. At least he acknowledged the transactional nature of their relationship rather than pretending it was something else.

"And what about what I want?" she asked, the question escaping before she could contain it.

Richard glanced at her, genuine confusion crossing his features. "You have everything you want, don't you? The penthouse, the clothes, the social position. Now the yacht trip."

Eliza let the question dissolve, recognizing it had no place in their carefully constructed arrangement. "Of course. I was just teasing."

His hand remained on her thigh, but the momentary connection had passed. They rode the rest of the way in silence, each retreating to familiar roles that required no uncomfortable introspection.

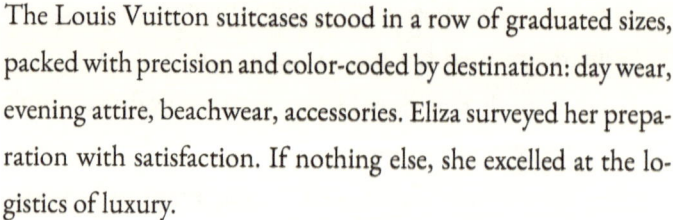

The Louis Vuitton suitcases stood in a row of graduated sizes, packed with precision and color-coded by destination: day wear, evening attire, beachwear, accessories. Eliza surveyed her preparation with satisfaction. If nothing else, she excelled at the logistics of luxury.

The penthouse felt unusually quiet, Richard having departed for a late meeting despite their early flight the next morning. Eliza wandered to the expansive windows, New York spread before her like a glittering promise she'd already collected on.

Her phone rang, interrupting her reverie. The screen displayed a name she rarely saw: MELISSA.

Eliza hesitated, finger hovering over the answer button. Her sister called perhaps twice a year—birthdays and Christmas—their conversations brief and laden with unspoken resentments. Why would she be calling now, the night before Eliza's departure?

Sighing, she accepted the call. "Melissa. This is a surprise."

"Hey, Liz." Her sister's voice carried the familiar slightly nasal quality Eliza remembered from childhood. No one else called her Liz anymore—the diminutive felt alien to her carefully crafted identity.

"Is everything alright?" Eliza asked, defaulting to the assumption that unexpected contact meant trouble.

"Everything's fine," Melissa replied. "Mom mentioned you're going on some fancy yacht trip, and I realized I still had those seahorse earrings you loved as a kid. Thought you might want them."

The mention of their mother triggered Eliza's defensive reflex. She maintained minimal contact with her family, sending generous checks on appropriate occasions while avoiding the messy entanglement of actual relationships.

"That's... thoughtful," she managed. "But we're leaving tomorrow morning."

"Right, of course." Melissa's voice cooled slightly. "Just thought I'd offer."

An uncomfortable silence stretched between them, filled with the ghostly echoes of shared childhood and divergent choices.

"How's Adam?" Eliza finally asked, referring to her sister's husband of eight years—a high school teacher with perpetually ink-stained hands and a laugh Eliza remembered as surprisingly genuine.

"He's good. Just got department chair, actually. And Cody made the honor roll this semester."

Cody—her nephew, whom she'd met exactly twice. Eliza felt a strange pang at the realization.

"That's wonderful," she said, and meant it. "Please congratulate them both for me."

Another silence, this one weighted with the unasked questions Melissa always seemed to carry: *Are you happy? Is all that money worth it? Do you ever regret your choices?*

"Mom says Richard is doing really well," Melissa offered, the statement somewhere between observation and accusation.

"Yes, his fund had an excellent quarter."

"That's not what I meant."

Of course it wasn't. Eliza moved away from the window, suddenly unable to bear the view of the city she'd been so determined to conquer.

"Melissa, is there something specific you wanted to discuss? I still have packing to finish."

Her sister sighed, the sound crackling through the connection. "No, Liz. I just... I saw those pictures you posted from that charity thing. You looked beautiful, but you also looked..."

"Looked what?" Eliza prompted when Melissa trailed off.

"Sad. You looked sad, Liz. Like when we were kids and you'd put on Mom's makeup and pretend to be someone else."

The observation landed like a slap. Eliza's grip tightened on the phone.

"I'm not sad," she replied, her voice cooling to the polite distance she maintained with acquaintances. "I have everything I could possibly want."

"Okay." Melissa's tone made it clear she didn't believe it. "Well, have a great trip. Send a postcard or something if you think of it."

"I will. Give my love to Adam and Cody."

After they disconnected, Eliza stood motionless in the center of her perfect penthouse, surrounded by luxury luggage packed for a dream vacation. The call had disrupted her careful compartmentalization, forcing unwelcome questions to the surface.

She wandered into their bedroom, opening the safe where her jewelry was stored. Among the Cartier and Bulgari pieces lay a small velvet box she rarely opened. Inside were the few items she'd kept from before—a silver locket from her grandmother, a charm bracelet from her sixteenth birthday, and a photograph.

The picture showed two young girls on a New Jersey beach, their sunburned faces split with genuine grins as they held up a collection of seashells. Eliza remembered that day—one of the rare occasions their mother had been sober enough to take them on an outing. Melissa had found a perfect sand dollar, and Eliza had discovered tiny seahorse earrings in a boardwalk shop.

She couldn't remember what had happened to those earrings. Somewhere in the desperate scramble of her early modeling days, they'd disappeared along with most other connections to her past. Now she knew Mellissa had them.

Closing the box, Eliza returned it to the safe. The momentary nostalgia served no purpose. She had made her choices deliberately, trading authentic connection for security and status. The fact that Melissa couldn't understand that bargain didn't make it any less valid.

Still, as Eliza moved through the silent penthouse, checking last-minute details for their trip, she found herself unusually restless. The glossy brochures with their promises of paradise lay on the coffee table, but the excitement she'd felt earlier had faded.

Richard still hadn't returned by midnight. Eliza slipped between the silk sheets alone, staring at the ceiling as sleep eluded her.

Tomorrow they would board a private jet to the Caribbean, where a luxury yacht awaited to carry them through turquoise waters to pristine beaches. She would wear her new resort wear, pose for perfect photographs, and perform her role as Richard's beautiful, enviable wife.

It was everything she had worked for, schemed for, married for.

Why, then, did she feel as empty as the space beside her in their king-sized bed?

Rolling onto her side, Eliza pushed the question away. Doubts were an indulgence she couldn't afford, not when she'd invested so much in this particular version of success.

Yet as sleep finally claimed her, her dreams were not of yacht decks and champagne sunsets, but of a New Jersey beach and the sound of her sister's laughter—a sound she hadn't heard in years.

CHAPTER THREE

Setting Sail

The St. Lucia marina gleamed like a showroom of excess, each vessel more extravagant than the last. White fiberglass and polished chrome reflected the Caribbean sun as uniformed staff scurried about, attending to the whims of those wealthy enough to inhabit this floating world of privilege. Sleek motor yachts with helicopter pads neighbored sailing vessels with masts that stretched toward the cloudless sky, their pristine decks populated by the tanned and beautiful.

Eliza stepped from the air-conditioned comfort of their private transfer, immediately grateful for the oversized Chanel sunglasses shielding her eyes from both the glare and the scrutiny of onlookers. She wore a white linen sundress that whispered against her skin, deliberately casual yet costing more than a month's salary for most of the staff bustling around them.

"Ah, there she is," Richard said, gesturing toward the end of the dock.

The Aurora awaited, 150 feet of gleaming perfection. Even among the extravagant vessels lining the marina, it commanded attention—sleek lines, multiple decks, and a hull painted a distinctive midnight blue that seemed to absorb light rather than reflect it.

A porter approached with their luggage cart, his smile professional and practiced.

"Allow me to assist with your bags, sir," he offered, reaching for the handle.

Richard withdrew a crisp hundred-dollar bill from his wallet, holding it just visible between his fingers. "Take special care with the leather pieces," he instructed, the bill remaining conspicuously unpresented until the man nodded his understanding.

"Of course, sir. Right away."

Only then did Richard release the bill, the transaction more about establishing hierarchy than rewarding service. Eliza had seen him perform this ritual countless times—the deliberate delay in tipping, the implication that service could be rewarded or withheld based on his whim. It was a performance of power she'd once found impressive but now viewed with a discomfort she carefully concealed.

As they followed the porter toward the yacht, a flurry of activity on the Aurora's deck caught Eliza's attention. A man was securing equipment with practiced efficiency, his movements economical and assured. Even from a distance, his physique was evident—broad shoulders tapering to a narrow waist, arms defined by functional strength rather than cosmetic gym routines.

Unlike the uniformed crew members, he wore faded cargo shorts and a simple t-shirt that had molded to his body through work and wear rather than designer tailoring. When he straightened, wiping his brow with his forearm, Eliza caught her first clear glimpse of his face—sun-darkened skin, strong jawline softened by a day's stubble, and eyes that seemed to take in everything around him with alert assessment.

The contrast between this man and her husband was impossible to ignore. Richard, despite his regular sessions with an exclusive personal trainer, carried the softness of someone whose greatest exertion came from golf swings and board meetings. His carefully maintained physique was decorative rather than functional, his manicured hands never having known genuine labor.

Beside her, Richard was speaking to the marina manager, his tone carrying that particular blend of cordiality and condescension he reserved for service interactions. Eliza maintained her attentive expression while her gaze drifted back to the deckhand, who had now noticed their approach.

For a moment, their eyes met across the distance. No smile, no acknowledgment—just an unfiltered appraisal that carried none of the deference she was accustomed to receiving from staff. Then he turned away, returning to his task with indifference that bordered on dismissal.

A strange flutter of irritation—or was it interest?—stirred in Eliza's chest. She was accustomed to being noticed, to commanding attention with her appearance. The man's apparent immunity to her presence was both novel and vaguely unsettling.

"Mrs. Harrington?" The marina manager addressed her directly, breaking her distraction. "Your luggage will be taken directly to your stateroom. Captain Reynolds is waiting to welcome you aboard."

Eliza smiled her practiced smile, slipping back into her role as Richard's elegant accessory. "Wonderful. We're so looking forward to the experience."

As they approached the boarding ramp, she placed her hand on Richard's arm in a gesture of affection that had long ago become automatic rather than genuine. From the corner of her eye, she caught the deckhand watching this performance with an expression that could only be described as knowing cynicism.

Something about his gaze made her feel exposed, as if he could see through the carefully constructed image she presented to the world. Eliza raised her chin slightly, refusing to acknowledge his scrutiny as Richard guided her onto the yacht that would be their home for the next three weeks.

◆◇◆

"Welcome aboard the Aurora." Captain Reynolds was the epitome of nautical authority—silver-haired, weather-lined face, and the perfect balance of professionalism and hospitality. "We're delighted to have you with us, Mr. and Mrs. Harrington."

The yacht's main deck was a study in understated luxury—teak floors polished to a soft glow, cream upholstery, and brass fixtures that gleamed in the afternoon sun. A uniformed steward appeared with champagne flutes on a silver tray as the captain began introductions.

"This is Sofia, our chief stewardess, who will be overseeing your comfort during your stay."

A slender woman with an efficient smile nodded respectfully. "Welcome aboard. If you need anything at all, please don't hesitate to ask."

"And this is Chef Andre, formerly of Le Bernardin in New York."

The chef, compact and precise in his white jacket, gave a slight bow. "I've reviewed your dietary preferences and prepared a special welcome dinner for this evening."

Richard nodded with the air of someone accustomed to such attention. "Excellent. I understand your bouillabaisse is particularly noteworthy."

"I hope it meets your expectations, sir."

Eliza maintained her pleasant expression as the introductions continued. First Officer, Engineer, Stewards—each more deferential than the last. Richard immediately established his position in the hierarchy, peppering his responses with references to other luxury vessels he'd chartered and minor suggestions for service improvements.

"And this is Marco Delgado, our second deckhand and safety officer," Captain Reynolds said as they moved to the outer deck. "Former Special Forces and maritime survival expert. There's not a situation at sea he can't handle."

The man Eliza had noticed earlier stood before them, now in a pristine white uniform that did nothing to diminish his physical presence. Up close, he was even more striking—dark hair cut short but not severely, features that might have belonged to a classical sculpture, and eyes a startling shade of gray-blue that reminded her of the ocean during a storm.

"Mr. Harrington, Mrs. Harrington," he acknowledged with a nod that contained the minimum required respect without crossing into subservience.

Richard extended his hand with the automatic gesture of someone used to being the most important person in any room. "Naval background, the captain mentioned?"

"Yes, sir. Eight years with Naval Special Warfare, followed by private maritime security." Marco's handshake was brief, his tone professional but not deferential. "I oversee safety protocols and assist with navigation, particularly in less charted areas."

His accent was subtle—a hint of something Mediterranean softening his precise English. When his gaze shifted to Eliza, she felt an unexpected warmth rise to her cheeks.

"Mrs. Harrington." He inclined his head slightly.

"Mr. Delgado." She extended her hand, surprised when he took it with a grip that was firm but not overwhelming. His palm was callused against her soft skin, the contrast sending an unexpected tingle up her arm.

Their eyes met, and Eliza was struck by the directness of his gaze. He looked at her—truly looked—without the typical response her beauty usually elicited in men. No dazzled appreciation, no hunger, no attempt to impress. Instead, she saw assessment and something like recognition, as if he'd cataloged her type immediately: trophy wife, decorative and pampered.

The realization both irritated and intrigued her.

"I hope you'll find your time aboard comfortable," he said, releasing her hand.

"I'm sure it will be memorable," Eliza replied, her social training providing the appropriate response even as her mind registered the unusual tension between them.

Richard had already moved on, questioning the captain about engine specifications and nautical details he would soon forget but felt compelled to inquire about. Marco stepped back, assuming parade rest with an unconscious military precision that emphasized the controlled power in his frame.

The contrast between the two men couldn't have been more pronounced. Richard, with his designer resort wear and carefully maintained tan, exuded the soft authority of wealth—power derived from possession rather than capability. Marco, despite the uniform that marked him as staff, radiated a physical confidence and competence that needed no external validation.

As the tour continued through the yacht's luxurious interior, Eliza found her attention repeatedly drawn to Marco's presence. He moved with the easy grace of someone completely at home in their physical body, comfortable in any environment. When technical questions arose about the yacht's capabilities, his responses were concise and knowledgeable, his manner suggesting that Richard's attempts to establish dominance through questioning were transparent and somewhat amusing.

In their stateroom—a masterpiece of luxury with panoramic windows and a king-sized bed that faced the ocean—Richard immediately began rearranging items to his preference, instructing Sofia on additional requirements while barely glancing at the spectacular view.

"Your husband seems to know exactly what he wants," Sofia observed diplomatically as she unpacked Eliza's designer resort wear.

"Always," Eliza agreed, moving to the window to watch the marina activity below. She spotted Marco on the deck, stripped of his formal uniform shirt as he secured equipment in the afternoon heat. The sun highlighted the defined muscles of his shoulders and back, skin bronzed by outdoor work rather than salon tanning beds.

He worked with focused efficiency, indifferent to his surroundings in a way that suggested comfort with his place in the world. There was something compelling about his self-contained competence, so different from the constant status signaling of Richard's circle.

"Will that be all, Mrs. Harrington?" Sofia's voice pulled her from her observation.

Eliza turned from the window, composing her features into a polite smile. "Yes, thank you. Everything looks perfect."

As Sofia departed, Richard emerged from the bathroom, already on his phone discussing market fluctuations with his office. The real world—his world—maintaining its hold despite their luxurious escape.

Eliza returned her gaze to the window, but Marco had disappeared from view, leaving her with an inexplicable sense of disappointment and a growing awareness that this voyage might present complexities she hadn't anticipated.

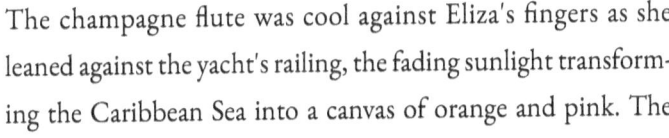

The champagne flute was cool against Eliza's fingers as she leaned against the yacht's railing, the fading sunlight transforming the Caribbean Sea into a canvas of orange and pink. The Aurora had departed the marina hours earlier, the coastline now a distant silhouette against the darkening sky.

"Another, Mrs. Harrington?"

Marco appeared beside her with a bottle, his uniform crisp once more, though he'd forgone the formal jacket in the evening heat. Up close, Eliza noticed a small scar bisecting his left eyebrow and the faint lines around his eyes that suggested he smiled more often than his current professional demeanor indicated.

"Please." She extended her glass, watching as he poured with practiced precision. "And it's Eliza, if you don't mind. 'Mrs. Harrington' makes me feel like my mother-in-law."

A hint of a smile touched his lips. "As you wish. Though Captain Reynolds runs a formal ship."

"Then we'll save it for when the captain isn't looking," she replied, surprising herself with the lightly flirtatious tone. The champagne was excellent but not strong enough to explain the sudden warmth in her cheeks.

Marco's expression revealed nothing beyond polite acknowledgment, but something in his eyes suggested he wasn't fooled by her casual charm.

"Your husband seems to be enjoying his calls more than the sunset," he observed, nodding toward where Richard paced the deck, gesturing emphatically into his satellite phone, his back to the spectacular natural display.

Eliza shrugged lightly. "Richard believes opportunities don't wait for vacations."

"And what do you believe, Mrs.—Eliza?"

The question caught her off guard. Service staff rarely asked about her beliefs or opinions, typically limiting conversation to safe topics like destinations or weather.

"I believe this champagne is excellent," she deflected, taking another sip.

Marco nodded, accepting her evasion with apparent under-standing. "Dom Pérignon Rosé, 2008. A good year." He stepped slightly closer to refill her glass, the movement bringing him within inches of her. The yacht chose that moment to crest a small wave, causing Eliza to sway toward him.

His hand steadied her elbow, the contact brief but electric through the thin silk of her evening dress. Up close, she caught his scent—clean salt air mingled with something woodsy and distinctly masculine.

"Easy," he murmured, his voice low. "You'll get your sea legs soon enough."

For a moment, they stood closer than social convention would dictate, his height requiring Eliza to tilt her face up to meet his gaze. The sunset painted his features in gold and am-ber, softening the hard lines of his jaw while illuminating the surprising intelligence in his eyes.

Eliza became acutely aware of her breathing, of the slight acceleration of her pulse that had nothing to do with the yacht's movement. With anyone else, she would have attributed the re-action to the champagne or the romantic setting, but she knew it was something more primal—an instinctive response to raw masculine energy so different from the cultivated sophistication she was accustomed to.

Marco stepped back first, resuming his professional distance as if the moment had never occurred. "The first night at sea is always the most magical," he said, his tone returning to that of a crew member addressing a guest. "If you're lucky, you might see phosphorescence in the water after dark."

Eliza gathered her composure, taking a deliberate sip of champagne. "Is that a recommendation from our safety officer?"

"A suggestion from someone who's spent enough nights at sea to know what's worth staying awake for." There was that hint of a smile again, gone almost before she could register it.

"Marco!" The captain's voice called from the bridge.

"Duty calls." He inclined his head slightly. "Enjoy your evening, Eliza."

As he walked away, Eliza found herself watching the confident stride that spoke of a man entirely comfortable in his own skin. She'd been surrounded by powerful men her entire adult life, but Marco's power was different—not derived from wealth or position but from capability and self-knowledge.

Richard continued his phone conversation, oblivious to both the magnificent sunset and his wife's wandering attention. Eliza turned back to the horizon, where the last sliver of sun was disappearing into the sea. The champagne tasted impossibly sweet on her tongue as she allowed herself a moment of fantasy—imagining what it might be like to be held by hands that had known real work, to be seen by eyes that weren't blinded by her decorative value.

The thought was inappropriate, unprofessional, and undeniably exciting. Eliza justified it as harmless imagination, the kind of fantasy any woman might indulge in when confronted with masculine beauty. It meant nothing—just a momentary diversion from the practiced performance of her real life.

Yet as darkness fell and the stars emerged in breathtaking clarity, she found her thoughts returning to Marco's steady gaze and the brief warmth of his hand on her arm. For the first time in years, Eliza felt something genuine stirring beneath her carefully maintained surface—curiosity, perhaps. Or hunger for something she'd forgotten she wanted.

Sleep eluded Eliza despite the gentle rocking of the yacht and the luxurious comfort of their stateroom. Richard slumbered beside her, having fallen into bed after a nightcap and several more business calls, barely acknowledging her presence beyond a perfunctory goodnight kiss.

Restless, she slipped from the sheets, wrapping herself in a silk robe before stepping onto their private deck. The night air caressed her skin, warm and salt-tinged. The moon cast a silver path across the water, an invitation to places unknown.

Deciding to explore the yacht while it was quiet, Eliza made her way through the main salon and toward the galley, thinking a glass of water might help her sleep. The vessel was different at night—more intimate, the polished surfaces gleaming softly in the low lighting.

She descended the curved staircase to the lower deck, realizing too late that she'd taken a wrong turn. Instead of the galley, she found herself in a narrow corridor she didn't recognize from the tour. Unsure which direction to turn, she continued forward, reasoning that any path must eventually lead somewhere familiar on a vessel of limited size.

The corridor narrowed further, and as Eliza rounded a corner, she collided with a solid form coming from the opposite direction. Strong hands grasped her upper arms to steady her, the contact shocking in its suddenness.

"I'm sorry, I didn't—" she began, then stopped as recognition dawned.

Marco stood before her, dressed in navy shorts and a simple white t-shirt that suggested he was off duty. In the confined space of the passageway, his height and breadth seemed even more imposing, his presence filling the available air.

"Mrs. Harrington," he said, surprise evident in his voice. "Are you lost?"

"Eliza," she corrected automatically, suddenly conscious of her thin robe and the nightgown beneath it. "And yes, I was looking for the galley."

"You're on the wrong deck." His hands released her arms, but the warmth of his touch lingered on her skin. "This is crew territory."

The corridor was narrow enough that there was barely space between them, the yacht's gentle motion occasionally causing their bodies to sway toward each other. Eliza caught that scent again—clean sweat mingled with something essentially masculine.

"I couldn't sleep," she explained unnecessarily. "I thought water might help."

Marco studied her face, his expression unreadable in the dim light. "The sea affects different people in different ways. Some find it soothing; others feel too much awareness of the vastness surrounding them."

The observation was surprisingly perceptive, hinting at depths beyond his professional role. Eliza found herself wanting to extend the conversation beyond the trivial.

"Which are you?" she asked.

A hint of surprise crossed his features, as if he hadn't expected genuine inquiry. "The sea is home to me. More than any land could be."

"That sounds like freedom," Eliza said, the words emerging before she could filter them.

Marco's expression shifted subtly, reassessing her with new-found interest. "It can be. Though some would consider it a prison—nowhere to go, limited space, at the mercy of the elements."

"Prisons come in many forms," she replied, again speaking with unusual candor. "Some have golden bars."

His eyes held hers, and for a moment Eliza felt truly seen—not as Richard Harrington's beautiful wife or as a wealthy client to be served, but as herself, with complexities and thoughts worthy of consideration.

"You surprise me," Marco said finally. "I wouldn't have expected philosophy in these passageways at midnight."

The comment carried an undercurrent that raised Eliza's defenses. "Because trophy wives don't typically engage in deep thought?"

Instead of retreating from her challenge, Marco leaned slightly closer, his voice lowering. "Because people reveal their true selves in unexpected moments, when the performance drops." His eyes held hers with uncomfortable directness. "You're different when he's not watching."

The observation struck too close to truth for comfort. Eliza straightened, calling upon years of social training to rebuild her composed façade. "I should return to my stateroom."

Marco didn't move immediately, maintaining the charged proximity between them. "I'll show you the way to the main deck."

He gestured for her to precede him, the narrow corridor forcing her to brush against him as she passed. The contact, though fleeting, sent an electric awareness through her body that had nothing to do with navigation and everything to do with the fundamental attraction between woman and man.

As they walked, Marco spoke again, his tone conversational but with an underlying current of challenge. "I served under an admiral once who had a theory about wealth. He said there are two types of rich people—those who've earned their fortune through work and understand the value of labor, and those who move paper around and believe money itself has inherent worth."

"And which category does my husband fall into?" Eliza asked, unable to resist the provocation.

Marco's smile was barely visible in the dim lighting. "I wouldn't presume to classify your husband, Mrs. Harrington."

"But you already have," she countered, stopping to face him in the corridor. "Just as you've classified me."

"Have I?" His eyes held a glint of something that might have been admiration for her directness.

"From the moment we boarded. I saw how you looked at us—at me." Eliza didn't know why she was pursuing this uncomfortable truth, only that something about this man made her want to strip away pretense.

Marco didn't deny it. "We all make assessments based on limited information. Sometimes we're wrong."

"And sometimes we're right," Eliza replied.

They had reached the staircase leading to the main deck. Marco paused, standing close enough that Eliza could feel the heat radiating from his body.

"The galley is through the salon, first door on your right," he said. "Or I can bring water to your stateroom if you prefer."

The offer was professional, but the undercurrent between them was anything but. Eliza was acutely aware of her night-clothes, of her bare feet on the polished deck, of how different she must appear from her carefully curated daytime image.

"Thank you, but I can manage." She gathered her robe more tightly around herself. "Goodnight, Mr. Delgado."

"Marco," he corrected, the ghost of a smile touching his lips. "Since the captain isn't looking."

Something about his easy confidence both irritated and attracted her—a man so comfortable with himself that he required no external validation, who saw through social performance with disturbing accuracy.

"Goodnight, Marco," she amended.

As she ascended the stairs, Eliza felt his eyes on her, the awareness prickling along her skin. Their encounter had lasted mere minutes but had somehow stripped away layers of artifice she typically maintained without effort.

Back in the stateroom, Richard hadn't stirred, his breathing deep and regular in the darkness. Eliza slipped into bed beside him, her body still humming with an energy she couldn't—or wouldn't—name.

She stared at the ceiling, where moonlight cast shifting patterns through the window. The yacht rocked gently beneath her, carrying them all toward unknown waters in more ways than one.

Sleep remained elusive, but Eliza no longer minded the wakefulness. Her mind replayed the encounter in the corridor—the surprising depth in Marco's eyes, the challenging intelligence in his observations, the undeniable current of attraction she had no business feeling.

It's nothing, she told herself firmly. *Just the novelty of the setting, the champagne, the romantic moonlight.*

Yet as she finally drifted toward sleep, it was Marco's face that followed her into dreams, not her husband's familiar features. And somewhere in the space between wakefulness and slumber, Eliza admitted a dangerous truth: for the first time in years, she felt genuinely alive, awakened by the unexpected connection with a man who saw through her carefully constructed façade to the woman hiding beneath.

Chapter Four

Choppy Waters

The Caribbean sun burned high overhead, transforming the Aurora's upper deck into a stage for the time-honored ritual of the wealthy at leisure. Eliza reclined on a cushioned lounger, her body glistening with oil that caught the light with every subtle movement. She'd chosen her swimwear with deliberate care that morning—a barely-there gold bikini that offered the minimum required coverage while maximizing impact. The Brazilian cut left little to the imagination, the fabric clinging to her curves like a possessive lover.

Richard hadn't noticed. He paced the shaded portion of the deck, satellite phone pressed to his ear, gesturing emphatically as he discussed market fluctuations with the office he'd supposedly left behind. His occasional glances toward Eliza were proprietary rather than appreciative—checking on his possession rather than admiring his wife.

Eliza was accustomed to his distraction, had even come to prefer it. His absence created space for her to breathe, to exist without performing the role of adoring spouse. She adjusted her position slightly, angling her body toward the sun, aware that her movements drew another gaze entirely.

Marco worked methodically on the forward deck, coiling ropes and checking equipment with the focused precision she'd come to associate with him. Though his attention remained primarily on his tasks, Eliza hadn't missed the occasional glance in her direction—quickly averted but unmistakable. Unlike the open leering she often received from men, his looks carried something more complex—appreciation tempered by restraint, desire held firmly in check by professionalism.

The awareness of his gaze sent a pleasant warmth through her that had nothing to do with the tropical sun. Eliza had spent her adult life being looked at, her appearance her primary currency in the economy of her marriage, yet Marco's subtle attention affected her differently. Perhaps because he seemed to be fighting it rather than freely indulging, or perhaps because when he did look at her, he seemed to see beyond the carefully maintained exterior to something more essential.

Reaching for her water bottle, Eliza deliberately arched her back slightly more than necessary, letting the movement showcase the smooth curve of her spine. From beneath her sunglasses, she watched Marco's reaction—the momentary stillness, the slight tightening of his jaw before he returned to his task with renewed focus.

The silent exchange carried a thrill she hadn't experienced in years. Not the practiced seduction she performed with Richard, nor the calculated flirtation she deployed at business dinners, but something more elemental—the ancient dance between woman and man, stripped of social complexity.

A sudden impulse seized her. Setting aside her water, Eliza reached for the suntan oil beside her lounger, then called out: "Marco? Could I trouble you for a moment?"

Richard continued his business call, oblivious to the undercurrents around him. Marco looked up, his expression carefully neutral as he approached her lounger.

"Yes, Mrs. Harrington?"

"Eliza," she corrected, sitting up to face him. His eyes remained steadfastly on her face, the discipline suggesting years of practiced restraint. "Would you mind?" She held out the oil bottle. "I can't quite reach my back."

A nearly imperceptible hesitation, then: "Of course."

He took the bottle, moving behind her as she turned to provide access to her back. Eliza felt a flutter of anticipation, knowing she was crossing an unspoken line but unable to resist the temptation to feel his hands on her skin.

The first touch sent a shock through her system—his strong fingers warm against her shoulders, made slick by the oil. Marco applied the lotion with efficient movements, maintaining a professional distance despite the intimacy of the task.

"You're very tense," he observed quietly, his fingers finding a knot at the base of her neck.

Eliza closed her eyes, suppressing a small sound of pleasure as his thumb worked against the tightness. "Hazard of New York living," she managed.

His hands moved lower, tracing the curve of her spine with careful attention. Each stroke sent ripples of awareness through her body, awakening nerve endings she'd forgotten she possessed. The physical sensation was pleasurable, but the forbidden nature of the exchange—a beautiful woman being touched by a man not her husband, mere feet from where that husband conducted business—heightened every sensation to an almost unbearable degree.

"The waters around these islands are some of the most remarkable in the world," Marco said conversationally, his tone belying the charged nature of their contact. "There's a reef system to the east that few tourists ever see."

Eliza recognized his attempt to normalize the moment, to provide conversational cover for what might otherwise be too revealing an exchange. She seized the lifeline gratefully.

"Have you explored it?" she asked, her voice steadier than she felt.

"Many times. The currents create unique formations—caverns and passages that seem designed by an architect rather than nature." His hands continued their devastating work, moving to her lower back where the strings of her bikini offered minimal interruption.

"You know a great deal about these waters," she observed, aware of how his thumbs traced the subtle indentations just above the curve of her hips.

"Navigation is a matter of life and death at sea," Marco replied. "Understanding currents, reading weather patterns—these aren't luxury skills out here. They're survival."

There was something in his tone—not lecture but genuine passion—that caught Eliza's interest beyond the distraction of his touch. She twisted slightly to look at him over her shoulder.

"Could you teach me something about it?"

Surprise flickered across his features, quickly replaced by consideration. "You're interested in navigation?"

"I'm interested in knowledge that matters," she replied with unexpected honesty. "As opposed to knowing which fork to use for the fish course or which designer is acceptable this season."

A genuine smile transformed his face, creating crinkles around his eyes that suggested it was a natural expression for him, if not one he displayed often in his professional capacity.

"I could show you the basics of chart reading, if you're serious."

"I am," Eliza confirmed, surprised to realize she meant it.

Marco recapped the oil bottle, his task complete though Eliza could still feel the phantom impression of his hands on her skin. "Tomorrow morning, before it gets too hot. The chart room has the best maps."

Eliza smiled, not the practiced expression she deployed at social functions but something more genuine. "I'll look forward to it."

"What will you look forward to, darling?" Richard's voice cut through their exchange as he approached, phone finally tucked away.

Eliza's smile shifted instantly to her wife-persona version. "Marco was just telling me about a reef system nearby. Apparently it's quite spectacular."

Richard cast a dismissive glance toward Marco. "I'm sure it is. We'll need fresh towels in the master suite, and my wife could use a refill on her water."

The abrupt shift to service requests—clearly intended to reestablish hierarchy—sent color rising to Eliza's cheeks. She caught herself almost apologizing to Marco for her husband's tone before remembering that such acknowledgment would only emphasize the awkwardness.

Marco's expression revealed nothing beyond professional accommodation. "Right away, sir." He turned to go, then added to Eliza, "The charts will be ready whenever you'd like to see them, Mrs. Harrington."

As he walked away, Eliza noticed how his shoulders had straightened, his posture shifting from relaxed conversation to rigid professionalism. She felt an unexpected pang of regret for the moment's disruption, for the glimpse of genuine connection so quickly severed.

Richard settled onto the lounger beside her, already checking messages on his phone. "The Tokyo markets opened strong," he remarked, as if continuing a conversation she'd been part of.

"How nice," Eliza murmured, her attention elsewhere.

Captain Reynolds appeared on deck, approaching with purpose. "Mr. Harrington, Mrs. Harrington," he greeted them. "I've just received the latest weather report. There's a tropical storm system developing to the southeast, moving in our direction."

Richard frowned, setting aside his phone. "How serious?"

"Serious enough that I'm recommending we alter course," the captain replied. "We can head northwest and avoid the worst of it. We'd need to skip St. Vincent but could make up the time at Martinique."

"Skip St. Vincent?" Richard's displeasure was evident. "That's where the exclusive cove is—the one the broker specifically highlighted. It's the reason we chose this itinerary."

"Safety must be our priority, sir," Captain Reynolds said firmly. "The storm could develop into something more significant. Standard protocol is to maintain a wide berth."

Richard waved a dismissive hand. "I've been through storms before. The Aurora can handle some choppy water."

Eliza watched the exchange with growing concern. "Perhaps we should listen to the captain's recommendation," she suggested carefully.

Richard's gaze flicked to her, brief annoyance crossing his features. "It's a tropical storm, not a hurricane. These luxury vessels are built to withstand far worse." He turned back to the captain. "How long before it reaches us?"

"Current projections have it intersecting our path by tomorrow evening, but these systems can accelerate unexpectedly."

"Then we have time to reach St. Vincent and spend the day there before continuing northwest," Richard concluded. "Best of both worlds."

Captain Reynolds's expression remained professional, but Eliza detected his disapproval. "I must emphasize, sir, that the prudent course would be—"

"I understand your concern," Richard interrupted, "but I've chartered this vessel at considerable expense specifically for this route. Unless you're telling me there's imminent danger, I'd prefer we maintain our original plan."

A tense silence followed. Eliza glanced toward the forward deck, where Marco had paused in his work, clearly listening to the exchange. His expression was unreadable, but something in his stance suggested controlled concern.

"Very well, sir," the captain finally conceded. "We'll continue to monitor the situation closely. If conditions worsen, we may need to reconsider."

As the captain departed, Eliza touched Richard's arm. "Is that wise? If they're concerned..."

"They're being overly cautious," Richard replied with the confidence of someone accustomed to bending the world to his preferences. "These crews always exaggerate weather concerns to cover themselves. Remember that Mediterranean charter where the captain wanted to skip Capri because of 'dangerous winds' that turned out to be nothing?"

"This seems different," Eliza persisted. "Maybe we should—"

"I didn't pay two hundred thousand dollars to miss the highlight of the trip," Richard cut her off, his tone final. "Now, shall we have lunch? I believe Sofia mentioned a seafood platter."

Eliza recognized the futility of further discussion. Richard had made his decision, as he always did, with the absolute certainty of a man who believed his wealth insulated him from consequences.

As they rose to move toward the dining area, she caught Marco watching them, his gaze meeting hers briefly across the deck. Something passed between them in that moment—a shared understanding, perhaps, or a premonition. Eliza felt a strange chill despite the tropical heat, a sense that the smooth waters around them concealed deeper currents neither of them could control.

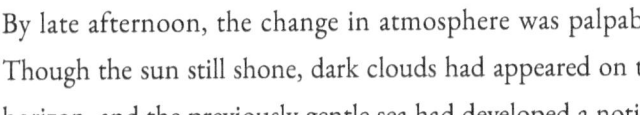

By late afternoon, the change in atmosphere was palpable. Though the sun still shone, dark clouds had appeared on the horizon, and the previously gentle sea had developed a noticeable chop. The Aurora's movements became more pronounced, a subtle roll that required adjustment when walking.

From her position on the salon deck, Eliza watched Marco and the first officer working systematically to secure loose items and prepare the yacht for rougher conditions. Marco moved with focused efficiency, muscles flexing beneath his t-shirt as he tightened straps and checked equipment. Despite the gravity of his task, there was something mesmerizing about his physical capability, the confidence with which he anticipated the vessel's needs.

In the salon behind her, Richard held court with Sofia and the chef, discussing dinner options with elaborate unconcern for the darkening horizon. He'd been drinking steadily since lunch, his voice growing louder as he dismissed the increasingly frequent weather updates from the bridge.

"Sir?" Sofia approached hesitantly. "Captain Reynolds suggests moving dinner forward by an hour. He believes conditions may deteriorate by later evening."

"Nonsense," Richard waved his hand, the motion sloshing scotch over the rim of his glass. "We'll dine at the usual time. Andre has prepared that special bouillabaisse, hasn't he? Needs proper appreciation."

Eliza turned from her observation of Marco to focus on her husband. "Richard, perhaps we should consider the captain's suggestion. The sea is already getting rougher."

Richard's expression hardened slightly. "Not you too. It's barely a swell. Stop letting them panic you over nothing."

The dismissal was typical, yet somehow more grating than usual. Perhaps because Eliza had glimpsed an alternative in her interactions with Marco—conversations where her input was considered rather than dismissed, where her thoughts were engaged rather than managed.

She returned her attention to the deck, where Marco was now securing the tender with additional lines. As if sensing her gaze, he looked up, meeting her eyes across the distance. For a moment they simply regarded each other, an unspoken communication passing between them.

Marco glanced toward the approaching storm clouds, then back to Eliza, his expression carrying clear warning. She nodded slightly, acknowledging his concern. Without words, they'd established an alliance of sorts, a recognition of reality that contrasted sharply with Richard's determined denial.

The yacht pitched suddenly, sending a decorative vase crashing to the deck. Sofia rushed to clean up the shattered pieces while Richard complained about the disruption to his drink.

"You might want to change into something more substantial," Marco suggested as he passed Eliza, nodding toward her light sundress. "And secure anything valuable in your stateroom. Just as a precaution."

"Thank you," she replied, lowering her voice. "Is it going to be bad?"

Marco's eyes shifted toward Richard, then back to her. "Let's just say I wouldn't be hosting a formal dinner tonight. The storm is accelerating faster than predicted."

The quiet confidence in his assessment, devoid of Richard's blustering certainty or the crew's diplomatic hedging, settled in

Eliza's chest with the weight of truth. She nodded, appreciating his directness.

"I'll change," she decided, moving toward the stairs to their stateroom.

As she descended, she heard Richard call after her, "Tell Sofia to bring more ice when you see her."

In their suite, Eliza exchanged her sundress for fitted jeans and a light sweater, securing her hair in a practical ponytail. The change felt symbolic somehow, a shift from decorative accessory to functional human. She tucked away her jewelry and secured their electronics in the cabin safe, instinctively preparing for what her husband refused to acknowledge.

When she returned to the main salon, the sky had darkened considerably, and the yacht's motion had intensified from gentle roll to pronounced pitch. Richard remained sprawled on the sofa, drink in hand, while Sofia hovered nearby, clearly concerned but unwilling to challenge his authority again.

"You've changed," Richard observed with mild surprise. "A bit casual for dinner, isn't it?"

"I thought something more practical might be appropriate, given the conditions," Eliza replied, steadying herself against a chair as the yacht crested a larger wave.

Richard's response was cut short by the captain's appearance. "Mr. Harrington," he began, his tone professionally firm, "I must insist we delay dinner and secure the vessel properly. The storm has intensified and changed direction. We're now directly in its path."

"Oh, for God's sake," Richard exclaimed, but even he couldn't deny the evidence of his senses as the yacht lurched sharply, sending his drink tumbling to the carpet. "Fine, fine. Do what you need to do."

Captain Reynolds nodded curtly. "Sofia will bring you both a light meal in your stateroom. I recommend you remain there until morning. We'll be experiencing significant motion for the next several hours."

As if to punctuate his warning, a crash of thunder sounded overhead, followed by the sudden drumming of rain on the deck. The transition from afternoon sun to storm had happened with startling speed, as if nature had tired of being ignored and decided to command attention.

"Come on," Eliza urged Richard, helping him to his feet. "Let's go below."

As they made their way toward the stairs, Marco appeared from the upper deck, rain gleaming on his skin and soaking his shirt. His eyes found Eliza's immediately.

"Secure everything in your room," he instructed, all pretense of deference gone in the face of practical necessity. "Use the handrails. The worst is still to come."

Richard bristled at the commanding tone. "Now see here—"

"Richard," Eliza interrupted firmly, "he's trying to help. Let's just do as he says."

Something in her voice—a certainty or authority she rarely displayed—gave Richard pause. He allowed her to guide him toward their stateroom, though not without a resentful glance back at Marco.

Behind them, Eliza heard rapid conversation between Marco and the captain, their tones urgent but controlled. The composed competence in Marco's voice contrasted sharply with Richard's petulant complaints as they descended the stairs, reinforcing Eliza's growing awareness of the gulf between the two men—one who commanded respect through capability, the other who demanded it through wealth.

In their stateroom, the motion was even more pronounced, the view through their panoramic windows now a chaotic scene of heaving waves and slashing rain. Sofia appeared with a tray of sandwiches and secured thermoses, moving with practiced efficiency despite the yacht's increasingly violent motion.

"The captain asks that you remain here," she advised, her professional calm belied by the tension around her eyes. "Use the bathroom with caution as the motion will intensify. There are grab bars installed beside the bed for your safety."

As she departed, Eliza caught her arm. "Is it very serious?"

Sofia hesitated, then replied with careful honesty, "Marco says it's escalated to near hurricane strength. We're in for a rough night, but the Aurora is a sturdy vessel." She patted Eliza's hand reassuringly before disappearing down the corridor.

"Overreacting, all of them," Richard muttered, though with less conviction than before. He settled on the edge of the bed, the motion of the yacht causing him to grip the covers for stability. "Should have brought the bottle with me."

Eliza secured the stateroom door and moved to the windows, watching as massive waves rose and fell in hypnotic rhythm. The yacht climbed each swell before plunging into the trough beyond, the cycle creating a disorienting sensation of perpetual falling.

"We should try to sleep," she suggested, knowing Richard's intoxication would make that easier for him than for her. "There's nothing to do but wait it out."

Richard didn't argue, his earlier bravado fading as the reality of their situation became impossible to ignore. He awkwardly prepared for bed, his movements hampered by both alcohol and the yacht's violent motion.

"Damned inconvenience," he mumbled as Eliza helped him into bed, securing the safety strap across the mattress as Sofia had shown them. "Still say they're overreacting."

Within minutes, his breathing had deepened into sleep, the combination of scotch and motion lulling him into unconsciousness despite the storm's growing fury. Eliza remained awake, watching the chaos beyond their windows with a strange, detached fascination.

The yacht's movements grew increasingly violent as the night progressed, objects sliding across surfaces despite being secured, the entire structure groaning under the assault of wind and wave. Eliza found herself thinking of Marco, imagining him moving confidently through the vessel, addressing problems with the calm competence she'd observed in him from the beginning.

The contrast between the luxury surrounding her and the raw power of nature outside created a surreal juxtaposition. All the wealth that typically insulated them from discomfort now seemed meaningless against the storm's indifferent rage. For perhaps the first time, Eliza felt the arbitrary nature of their privilege—how quickly the veneer of control could be stripped away by forces beyond their influence.

A particularly violent wave struck the yacht broadside, sending a decorative vase crashing to the floor despite its securing straps. Richard stirred but didn't wake, his breathing still deep and untroubled.

Eliza envied his oblivion as the storm intensified, transforming their floating palace into a fragile shell at the mercy of elemental forces. She found herself remembering Marco's hands on her shoulders that morning—steady, capable, reassuring. The memory provided strange comfort amid the chaos, as if his touch had somehow transferred a portion of his confidence to her.

As rain lashed the windows and thunder boomed overhead, Eliza surrendered to the violent rhythm of the storm, acknowledging her powerlessness while finding unexpected freedom in the recognition. All the careful control she maintained over her appearance, her behavior, her very identity—none of it mattered against the storm's fury.

She closed her eyes, not expecting sleep but wanting to rest before whatever morning might bring. The last thought before exhaustion finally claimed her was of Marco—not his physical appeal but his centered certainty, the sense that he knew exactly who he was regardless of circumstance. It was a quality she had never possessed and suddenly, desperately wanted to understand.

A tremendous crash jolted Eliza from sleep, consciousness returning with disorienting suddenness. The stateroom was in darkness save for the emergency lighting, casting eerie shadows across unfamiliar angles. The yacht's motion had transformed from rhythmic pitching to violent lurching, accompanied by the shriek of alarms and the unmistakable sound of water rushing somewhere nearby.

"Richard!" She reached for her husband, but another violent movement threw her from the bed onto a floor that tilted at an impossible angle.

The impact drove the breath from her lungs. Gasping, Eliza struggled to orient herself in the chaotic darkness. A flash of lightning illuminated the stateroom, revealing furniture torn from its moorings and water beginning to seep under the door.

"Richard, wake up!" she called again, crawling toward the bed where her husband remained strapped in, stirring groggily.

"What's happening?" he mumbled, his voice thick with sleep and lingering intoxication.

"We need to move," Eliza urged, releasing his safety strap. "Something's wrong with the yacht."

As if confirming her assessment, a shuddering impact reverberated through the vessel, accompanied by the sickening sound of tearing metal. The tilting floor suddenly dropped further, sending Eliza sliding toward the far wall.

"My God," Richard gasped, finally comprehending their situation. He tried to stand but immediately lost his footing, falling heavily against the nightstand.

A pounding at their door preceded its violent opening, revealing Marco silhouetted against the emergency lighting of the corridor. He was soaked, a cut bleeding freely across his forehead, but his voice carried the same steady authority Eliza had come to associate with him.

"We need to evacuate," he announced without preamble. "The yacht's taking on water. Grab only essentials—documents, medications. Nothing else."

Richard stared at him in disbelief. "Evacuate? In this storm? That's insane!"

"Staying is suicide," Marco countered, moving into the room to help Eliza to her feet. His hand closed around her arm with firm gentleness, steadying her against the yacht's violent motion. "The hull's been breached. We have minutes, not hours."

The certainty in his voice cut through Richard's protests. Eliza moved immediately to the safe, retrieving their passports and a small waterproof case where she kept essential medications.

"What about—" Richard began, gesturing toward their luggage.

"Nothing else," Marco interrupted. "Life vests are outside. Follow me. Stay low and keep one hand on the wall at all times."

The corridor beyond their stateroom had transformed into a nightmare landscape of tilted perspectives and intermittent lighting. Water sloshed around their ankles, rising visibly with each passing second. Other members of the crew moved with urgent purpose, life vests already secured.

Marco handed them each a vest from a nearby locker. "Put these on now," he instructed. "Secure all straps. Double-check each other."

Eliza fastened her vest with trembling fingers, then helped Richard with his, noting the fear that had replaced his usual confidence. Marco checked both vests with quick, practiced movements, his hands lingering a fraction longer on Eliza's shoulders than strictly necessary—a brief, reassuring pressure.

"The tender's been damaged," he explained as he led them toward the upper deck. "We're deploying life rafts. Stay together and do exactly as I say."

The journey through the crippled yacht was like moving through a fever dream. Familiar spaces had become alien, luxury rendered absurd by disaster. A priceless artwork hung at a bizarre angle, partially submerged in rising water. Crystal glasses shattered underfoot, mixing with seawater to create treacherous footing.

When they finally reached the deck, the full fury of the storm assaulted them with physical force. Rain lashed horizontally, driven by winds that threatened to tear them from their feet.

The darkness was near absolute, broken only by emergency lighting and the occasional stark illumination of lightning.

Through the chaos, Eliza made out a large inflatable raft from the side of the listing yacht.

"You first," Marco shouted to Eliza, guiding her toward the deployment area. "When I give the word, slide down the chute into the raft. Don't jump, don't hesitate."

Richard grabbed her arm. "I'm not getting in that thing! It's suicide in these waves!"

"Your choice is drowning here or having a chance out there," Marco replied bluntly. "The yacht is sinking. There is no third option."

A massive wave crashed over the deck, nearly sweeping Eliza off her feet. Only Marco's firm grip kept her upright, his body shielding her from the worst of the impact.

"Now!" he shouted as a momentary lull created better conditions. "Go!"

Eliza didn't hesitate. Detaching Richard's grip from her arm, she moved to the evacuation chute and let herself slide into the darkness below. The journey lasted seconds but felt eternal, ending with a jarring impact as she landed in the raft.

The raft bucked wildly on the massive waves, its connection to the yacht the only thing preventing it from being swept immediately away.

Above, lightning illuminated Richard's terrified face as Marco urged him toward the chute. Even from below, Eliza could see her husband's panic, his body rigid with fear as he shook his head in desperate denial.

Marco shouted something Eliza couldn't hear, then physically guided Richard to the chute, his superior strength overcoming the older man's resistance. Richard disappeared into the tube, emerging seconds later in the raft with a cry of terror.

Eliza reached for him instinctively, helping to secure him beside her. Richard's face was ashen, his breathing rapid and shallow with shock.

On deck, Marco exchanged rapid communication with the captain, then turned toward the evacuation chute. Lightning illuminated his descent, his controlled movements a stark contrast to Richard's panicked tumble.

He landed with practiced precision, immediately moving to help secure the final connections. Only when he knelt beside Eliza did she notice the blood still flowing from the cut on his forehead, mixing with rain to create pale rivulets down his face.

"Are you alright?" she shouted over the storm's fury.

His eyes met hers, surprise flickering briefly at her concern before he nodded. "Fine. Hold on to the straps—this will get worse before it gets better."

As if acknowledging his warning, a massive wave lifted the raft, straining the lines connecting it to the dying yacht. Through the darkness, Eliza could see the Aurora listing heavily to one side, its once-proud profile now a broken silhouette against the storm-tossed sky.

"Cut the lines!" Marco ordered, and quickly slashed through the connections with emergency knives.

Instantly, the raft was at the mercy of the sea, spinning away from the yacht's protective bulk into the full fury of the open ocean. Waves towered above them before crashing down with stunning force, sending water cascading over the raft's occupants.

Eliza clutched the safety straps with numbed fingers, her body pressed against Richard's rigid form. Across the raft, Marco worked to deploy the small stabilizing anchor, his movements sure despite the violent motion.

A particularly massive wave lifted the raft nearly vertical before slamming it back to the surface. Richard retched miserably, his expensive dinner returning to the sea that had claimed their luxury vessel. Eliza held him, murmuring reassurances that were lost to the storm's howl.

When she looked up, Marco was watching them, his expression unreadable in the intermittent lightning. Their eyes held across the chaos—his steady, hers wide with fear yet determined. Something passed between them in that moment, a recognition that transcended words: whatever came next, they would face it together.

Behind them, a tremendous groaning sound drew all eyes back to the Aurora. The yacht's stern was visibly sinking, the bow rising at an impossible angle before the entire vessel shuddered and began its final descent.

Eliza watched in stunned silence as millions of dollars of luxury disappeared beneath the waves, swallowed by an ocean indifferent to human concepts of value and status. All the carefully curated trappings of their privileged existence—gone in moments, leaving them as vulnerable as any creatures caught in nature's fury.

Marco moved closer, positioning himself beside Eliza and Richard. "Stay low," he instructed, his voice carrying that same steady certainty despite their dire circumstances. "We need to conserve energy and stay warm. The storm will pass by morning."

"And then what?" Richard demanded, his voice cracking. "We're in the middle of nowhere!"

"Then we survive," Marco replied simply. "One challenge at a time."

His shoulder pressed against Eliza's, warm despite their soaked clothing. She found herself leaning into that strength, drawing courage from his absolute focus on the present moment.

As the raft rose and fell on waves that gradually began to diminish, Eliza realized that everything had changed. The careful social divisions that had governed their interaction were meaningless now. Rich or poor, guest or crew—the sea recognized no such distinctions.

Morning would bring new challenges, but in this moment, adrift between the old world and whatever awaited them, Eliza felt strangely, terrifyingly free. Her fingers brushed against Marco's as they both held the same safety strap, the contact brief but electric even amid disaster.

He didn't pull away. Neither did she.

Around them, the storm began to exhaust itself, the worst of its fury spent. But within Eliza, something was just beginning to awaken—something that had nothing to do with the luxury she'd lost and everything to do with the man beside her, whose steady presence promised not comfort but something far more valuable: the truth of who she might become when stripped of everything she'd once believed defined her.

Chapter Five

Shipwreck

The night seemed eternal, a darkness pierced only by occasional lightning that illuminated their desperate situation in stark, terrifying flashes. The inflatable raft bucked and plunged on waves that gradually diminished from mountainous to merely threatening as the storm slowly exhausted its fury. What remained of the Aurora had long since disappeared beneath the churning waters, taking with it all the certainties of Eliza's previous life.

Their situation had grown more dire with each passing hour. Shortly after abandoning ship, a massive wave had swept Captain Reynolds and two crew members overboard, their cries fading quickly in the howling wind. Desperate attempts to locate them had proven futile, leaving only Eliza, Richard, and Marco to face the merciless sea.

Through it all, Marco had been their anchor. He hadn't rested, moving continuously around the small raft, adjusting the sea anchor, bailing water, and checking their position with a small GPS device he'd managed to keep functional despite the punishing conditions. His face, illuminated briefly during lightning flashes, showed exhaustion but never surrender, his movements economical yet effective despite hours of grueling exertion.

Richard had collapsed into misery almost immediately, seasickness rendering him worse than useless. He huddled against the raft's side, retching miserably until nothing remained but painful dry heaves. Occasional moans punctuated his suffering, his typical commanding presence entirely obliterated by physical distress.

Eliza surprised herself. After the initial shock had passed, she'd found reserves of strength she hadn't known she possessed. When Marco called for help securing the raft's cover against a particularly violent wave, she'd responded immediately, working beside him with an intuitive understanding of what needed to be done.

"Hold this," Marco instructed, passing her the emergency bailing cup while he checked their position for the hundredth time. Their fingers brushed in the exchange, the brief contact sending unexpected warmth through Eliza's chilled body.

"Any change?" she asked, her voice hoarse from hours of salt spray exposure.

Marco's expression remained carefully neutral. "We've drifted approximately twenty-two nautical miles southeast from our last position. The emergency beacon is still transmitting."

The unspoken reality hung between them: the Aurora had diverted from its registered course at Richard's insistence. The storm had scattered any nearby vessels. Rescue, if it came, would not be immediate.

The night crawled forward in this pattern—Eliza and Marco working in surprisingly synchronized tandem to keep their fragile craft afloat while Richard drifted in and out of miserable consciousness. Something fundamental had shifted in those dark hours, though Eliza couldn't have named it precisely. The artificial hierarchy that had governed their interactions aboard the yacht had dissolved, replaced by the more elemental currency of capability and will.

"You should rest," Marco told her during a brief lull in the waves' assault. "I can manage."

Eliza shook her head, rainwater streaming from her tangled hair. "I'm fine." The simple statement contained a truth she was only beginning to recognize—that she was indeed far stronger than anyone, including herself, had previously believed.

Marco studied her face for a moment, his expression unreadable in the darkness. Then he nodded once, acceptance rather than acquiescence, as if confirming something he'd suspected about her all along.

Their vigil continued through the endless night, the raft gradually finding smoother waters as the storm moved west-

ward. Sometime in those final dark hours, Eliza found herself
sitting shoulder-to-shoulder with Marco, their bodies pressed
together by necessity in the crowded space. The contact should
have been uncomfortable—inappropriate even—yet she found
herself drawing strength from his solid presence, from the
steady rise and fall of his breathing beside her.

"Dawn soon," Marco murmured, his voice close to her ear as
he checked the gradually lightening eastern horizon. "First light
will tell us what we're facing."

The simple pragmatism of his observation struck Eliza as
profoundly comforting. No false reassurances, no exaggerated
optimism, just clear-eyed assessment of their situation. It was
a stark contrast to the carefully crafted social platitudes she
was accustomed to exchanging, where truth was secondary to
appearance.

As the first gray light of dawn infiltrated the night sky, Marco
suddenly straightened, his gaze fixed on the horizon.

"Land," he said quietly, pointing toward a dark silhouette
against the lightening sky. "Two points off the port side."

Eliza squinted through the misty dawn, hope surging as she
made out the unmistakable profile of an island rising from the
sea. "How far?"

"Three miles, maybe four." Marco was already shifting to
adjust their trajectory, using a small emergency paddle to angle
their drift. "The current's carrying us close. We'll need to paddle
when we get closer to shore."

Richard stirred from his miserable stupor at their changed tone, struggling to sit upright. "Island? Where?"

"There," Eliza pointed, unable to keep the relief from her voice. "Marco says we're drifting toward it."

Richard squinted weakly at the horizon. "Well, thank God for that. There must be a resort, people who can contact my office—"

"It's not that kind of island," Marco interrupted, his tone factual rather than condescending. "From the profile, it's one of the smaller Grenadines. Uninhabited, most likely."

"Uninhabited?" Richard's voice cracked with disbelief. "That's ridiculous. Every island in the Caribbean has been developed."

Marco didn't argue, his attention already focused on calculating their approach. "The current's favorable, but we'll need to paddle through the surf break. All of us."

His gaze met Eliza's, a silent communication passing between them that required no words. She nodded, understanding both the necessity and the challenge ahead. Richard's protest died on his lips as the reality of their situation became impossible to deny.

As the sun crept above the horizon, burning away some of the lingering cloud cover, their target grew steadily larger. The relatively shallow water surrounding the island created breaking waves that tossed the raft with renewed violence, threatening to push them parallel to the shore rather than toward it.

"Now!" Marco called, thrusting a small emergency paddle into Richard's hands and taking the other himself. "We paddle on three!"

Richard fumbled with the paddle, his movements unco-ordinated and ineffective. Eliza positioned herself beside him, adding her strength to his efforts, guiding his motions with her own as Marco counted cadence from the raft's opposite side.

The next hour became a blur of exhausting effort. Each wave threatened to overturn them, each successful crest bringing the tantalizing shore closer yet still frustratingly distant. Eliza's muscles burned with exertion, her hands blistering on the paddle's rough surface, yet she continued with a determination that came from some previously untapped well of inner strength.

Marco remained their guiding force, his voice steady as he called instructions, his powerful strokes compensating for Richard's increasingly feeble efforts. When a massive wave near-ly capsized them, it was Marco who restored balance, his body moving with intuitive understanding of the water's rhythm.

"We're entering the surf break," he called as the waves grew steeper, the sound of breaking water now a constant roar. "When I say jump, we all go over the side. Swim hard for shore. The raft won't make it through the breakers."

"Jump?" Richard's voice rose in panic. "Into that?"

"It's our only chance," Marco replied, his tone allowing no argument. "The current will carry the raft away if we miss this approach."

Eliza met Marco's eyes across the heaving raft, a moment of silent communication passing between them. She would follow his lead, trusting his judgment in a way she'd never trusted Richard's despite years of marriage.

"Ready!" Marco shouted as a massive wave lifted them high. "Three, two, one—JUMP!"

Eliza launched herself over the raft's edge without hesitation, plunging into water so cold it stole her breath. The wave's force tumbled her, disorienting her completely until strong hands caught her arm, pulling her toward the surface.

Marco's face appeared beside her as they broke through. "Swim!" he ordered, already pulling her toward shore with powerful strokes.

Eliza fought through the churning water, focusing only on the next stroke, the next breath. Richard floundered nearby, his movements panicked and inefficient. Marco repeatedly adjusted their course, one arm supporting Eliza while the other reached for Richard, somehow managing to guide them both through waves that seemed determined to reclaim them for the sea.

The moment Eliza's feet touched sand remains forever imprinted in her memory—the sudden shift from helpless drifting to solid connection, from passive surrender to active control. She staggered forward, falling repeatedly as waves broke against her back, but each time she rose, moving closer to the beach beyond the surf.

Marco appeared beside her, one arm around Richard's waist, half-dragging his semi-conscious form through the shallows.

Together, they fought the last yards to shore, collapsing finally onto wet sand beyond the reach of all but the most ambitious waves.

For long moments, none of them spoke, their bodies pressed to the earth as if attempting to absorb its blessed solidity through skin. Eliza felt the rise and fall of her chest against the sand, each breath a miracle, each heartbeat a defiance of the death that had so nearly claimed them.

The rising sun broke fully through the clouds, bathing them in golden morning light that transformed the beach into a scene of unexpected beauty. White sand stretched in a gentle curve, leading to dense tropical vegetation beyond. No signs of human habitation were visible in either direction. Their only possessions were the clothes on their backs and whatever Marco had managed to secure in the waterproof pouch still strapped to his waist.

When she finally found strength to lift her head, Eliza saw Marco already rising to his knees, scanning their surroundings with tactical assessment. Richard remained prone, his breathing labored but stable.

"We made it," she whispered, the simple statement encompassing so much more than the physical journey from water to land.

Marco's eyes met hers, something like pride flickering in their depths. "You did well," he said simply. "Better than many trained sailors I've known."

The compliment, so different from the empty flattery she typically received about her appearance or charm, warmed something deep inside Eliza. She had been tested and not found wanting—perhaps for the first time in her adult life.

Richard groaned, rolling onto his back, his expensive resort wear now reduced to salt-crusted rags that hung from his frame like sad reminders of status rendered meaningless.

"Where the hell are we?" he managed, voice barely audible above the continuing surf.

"One of the smaller islands in the Grenadines," Marco replied, already moving with purpose despite his obvious exhaustion. "Uninhabited, from the look of it."

"That's impossible," Richard insisted, struggling to sit up. "There must be a resort, a fishing village, something..."

"There isn't." Marco's tone held absolute certainty. "This isn't a tourist destination. These smaller islands are nature preserves or privately owned, visited maybe once or twice a year by researchers or caretakers."

The implications settled over them slowly—no immediate rescue, no civilization, no comfort beyond what they could create from the island itself. Eliza watched understanding dawn on Richard's face, his expression shifting from disbelief to horror to a kind of frozen denial.

"We need to assess our situation," Marco continued, practical focus overriding exhaustion. "Fresh water is the priority. Shelter second. I'm going to check the tree line."

He rose to his feet with visible effort, his soaked clothing clinging to a body shaped by functionality rather than aesthetics. Despite hours of punishing exertion, he moved with determined purpose, already adapting to their new reality while Richard remained frozen in disbelief.

Eliza found herself rising to follow Marco, her body responding before conscious thought. "I'll help," she said simply.

Marco's brief glance held surprise and something else—respect, perhaps, or recognition of a kindred pragmatism he hadn't expected from a woman he'd first categorized as merely decorative.

"Richard needs to rest," she added, glancing back at her husband, who had collapsed again onto the sand, one arm flung across his eyes as if to block out the reality confronting them.

Marco nodded once, accepting her assessment and her assistance without question. As they walked toward the tree line, Eliza became acutely aware of the transformed dynamic between them. On the yacht, their interactions had been governed by rigid social hierarchy—wealthy client and service staff, each role carefully defined and maintained. Now, that artificial structure had dissolved, replaced by the more fundamental currency of capability.

The shift was both disorienting and strangely liberating. For the first time in years, Eliza was being evaluated not for her beauty or social grace but for her actual contributions. The realization straightened her spine despite bone-deep exhaustion, adding purpose to her steps as she followed Marco into the island's interior.

By late afternoon, the sun had fully established its dominance, burning away the last remnants of the storm clouds and baking their sodden clothes against their skin. Marco had located a small freshwater stream about half a mile inland, confirming the water was safe through methods Eliza would have dismissed as primitive survival-show nonsense just days earlier but now watched with rapt attention.

"We're lucky," he explained as they returned to the beach, carrying water in large leaves folded into makeshift cups. "This island has good water sources. Without that, we'd have three days at most."

"And with it?" Eliza asked, the practical question emerging naturally.

"Indefinite survival is possible. The ocean provides protein. There appear to be edible fruits and roots. The climate is forgiving." His assessment was clinical but held underlying optimism that Eliza found herself clinging to.

Richard had barely moved during their absence, his initial shock seemingly hardening into a kind of stubborn denial. He accepted the water without thanks, gulping it greedily before demanding, "What's the rescue plan? Surely that GPS thing still works."

Marco's expression remained neutral as he extracted the device from his waterproof pouch. "The emergency beacon continues transmitting our position. Given the storm's disruption to shipping lanes and the fact that we diverted from our registered course..." He paused, choosing his words carefully. "We should prepare for the possibility of extended waiting."

"Extended?" Richard's voice rose sharply. "How extended?"

"Days. Possibly weeks."

"Weeks?" Richard struggled to his feet, swaying slightly. "That's completely unacceptable. I have meetings, commitments. Do you have any idea what my time is worth?"

The absurdity of the question in their current circumstances hung in the air between them. Eliza watched Marco's face, seeing the barest flicker of contempt before his expression smoothed into professional neutrality.

"I understand this is difficult," Marco replied, his tone deliberately even. "Right now, we need shelter before nightfall. The temperature drops considerably after dark on these islands."

Without waiting for Richard's response, he turned his attention to the debris that had washed ashore from the yacht—splintered wood, torn fabric, fragments of once-luxurious furnishings now reduced to potential survival materials. With methodical efficiency, he began sorting through the wreckage, identifying pieces that could serve structural purposes.

Eliza joined him without being asked, her society manicure ruined as she dug through sand to retrieve a long piece of teak that had once been part of the Aurora's elegant decking. There was something strangely satisfying about the work—immediate, necessary, connected to actual survival rather than social performance.

Richard watched them from a distance, his expression a mix of disbelief and resentment at the transformed dynamic. In their previous life, Marco would have been invisible service staff, and Eliza would have been directing that staff from comfortable remove. Now she worked alongside Marco as a partner, while Richard remained sidelined by his own inability to contribute meaningfully.

"Richard, could you help gather some of the smaller pieces?" Eliza called, attempting to include him in the survival effort.

His response was a dismissive wave. "I'm strategizing our extraction. Someone needs to think beyond primitive shelters."

Eliza exchanged glances with Marco, reading in his eyes the same assessment she'd reached: Richard was worse than useless in their current situation—an active drain on limited resources rather than a contributor. The realization should have disturbed her more than it did.

As sunset approached, Marco had constructed a surprisingly sturdy lean-to shelter against a cluster of palms just beyond the beach. Using salvaged yacht debris, palm fronds, and knowledge that seemed to flow from instinct rather than conscious thought, he created a space that would protect them from dew and wind, if not from the psychological impact of their circumstances.

"It's not the Ritz," he acknowledged as Eliza helped secure the final lashings, "but it will keep us dry."

"It's impressive," she replied sincerely. "Where did you learn to do this?"

Something like a genuine smile touched his lips briefly. "Naval special operations. We trained for survival in every environment—desert, jungle, arctic, sea. You'd be surprised what the human body can endure with proper knowledge."

The simple statement carried implications that sent an unexpected shiver through Eliza. She found herself studying Marco with new awareness—not just his physical capability, which had been evident from their first meeting, but the depth of knowledge and experience that lay beneath his previously subservient role.

This man, who had silently served drinks and followed Richard's petulant orders aboard the yacht, possessed skills that meant the difference between life and death in their current reality. The reversal was so complete it bordered on mythic—the servant revealed as the secret king, the true authority emerging only when artificial structures fell away.

As darkness descended, the temperature dropped as Marco had predicted. The three gathered beneath the shelter, their bodies creating a small pocket of warmth in the rapidly cooling air. Marco had managed to start a small fire near the entrance using a waterproof lighter from his emergency pouch and skills Eliza had only seen in adventure films.

The flickering light cast dramatic shadows across their faces, highlighting the changed dynamic between them. Richard sat slightly apart, his expression closed and distant as he stared into the flames. Marco sat cross-legged at the shelter's entrance, his posture relaxed yet alert, like a sentinel guarding against unseen threats. Eliza found herself positioned between them—physically and metaphorically—her body drawn toward Marco's warmth and capability while her social conditioning still tethered her to Richard's side.

"We should discuss rationing," Marco said, breaking the heavy silence. "The emergency pouch contains minimal supplies. We'll need to forage tomorrow, establish a sustainable food source."

"Surely we'll be rescued before that becomes necessary," Richard interjected, his tone suggesting he could make it true through sheer force of will.

Marco met his gaze steadily across the fire. "We should prepare for all scenarios. Hope for rescue tomorrow, plan for survival beyond that."

The pragmatic approach struck Eliza as not just sensible but somehow profound—a philosophy for life distilled to its essence. She found herself nodding agreement, earning a briefly approving glance from Marco that sent warmth spreading through her chest despite the chill air.

As the fire burned lower, the reality of their sleeping arrangement became unavoidable. The shelter Marco had constructed was admirably sturdy but necessarily compact. Survival would require sharing body heat through the night—an intimacy forced by circumstance rather than choice.

"We should sleep close together," Marco stated, practical rather than suggestive. "Conserve body heat. The ground will draw warmth away quickly."

Richard's expression tightened with displeasure, but even he couldn't deny the logic. With visible reluctance, he positioned himself against the back wall of the shelter, leaving space for Eliza beside him.

Eliza hesitated, suddenly acutely aware of her body in a way that had nothing to do with her usual careful self-monitoring. Her soaked clothes had dried into salt-stiffened discomfort against her skin. Her hair, normally a point of pride, hung in tangled ropes around her face. Yet as Marco's eyes met hers across the dying fire, she felt a strange vulnerability that had nothing to do with physical appearance and everything to do with the person emerging from beneath her carefully constructed façade.

"I'll take first watch," Marco said, misinterpreting her hesitation. "We should maintain vigilance until we're more familiar with the island."

The suggestion of external threat provided convenient cover for the more complicated internal landscape Eliza was navigating. She nodded gratefully and settled beside Richard, who immediately turned his back to her, curling into himself both physically and emotionally.

Despite bone-deep exhaustion, sleep remained elusive as Eliza lay in the darkness. Behind her, Richard's breathing eventually deepened into the rhythm of unconsciousness. Before her, silhouetted against the night sky, Marco's outline remained vigilant, his posture suggesting he could maintain watch indefinitely through sheer force of will.

The events of the past twenty-four hours replayed in her mind like scenes from someone else's life. The luxury yacht, the storm, the desperate fight for survival—all of it felt simultaneously immediate and impossibly distant, as if she'd stepped through some portal into an alternate reality where different rules applied.

Yet amid the disorientation, Eliza recognized a strange clarity emerging. Stripped of designer clothes, deprived of cosmetics and social scripts, removed from the carefully constructed world of wealth and status, she was discovering something unexpected: a woman she barely recognized yet somehow knew had always existed beneath the surface.

This woman could help construct a shelter from debris, could swim through crushing waves, could face the stark reality of survival without collapse. This woman valued Marco's quiet competence over Richard's hollow posturing, recognized true strength when confronted with it rather than the artificial power conferred by wealth.

The realization was simultaneously terrifying and exhilarating. As if sensing her restless thoughts, Marco turned slightly, his profile catching the moonlight that filtered through the shelter's open side.

"Try to rest," he said softly, his voice carrying in the night stillness. "Tomorrow will require strength."

The simple statement contained neither condescension nor command, just recognition of shared challenge. Eliza found herself responding to that tone—not the practiced social response she'd perfected over years of marriage, but something more genuine.

"Thank you," she whispered, the words encompassing far more than gratitude for his current vigilance. "For everything today."

Marco nodded once, acknowledgment rather than dismissal of her gratitude. In the moonlight, with salt dried on his skin and exhaustion evident in the set of his shoulders, he looked more elementally masculine than any polished businessman she'd ever encountered at Richard's social functions. There was something compelling about his unadorned capability, his complete comfort in his own skin despite circumstances that would break lesser men.

As sleep finally began to claim her, Eliza's last conscious thought was surprisingly clear amid the chaos of their situation: the structures and values that had defined her existence for years had been swept away in a single night, revealing truths about herself—and the men beside her—that could never be unknown again.

Whatever came next, she was already irrevocably changed by the revelation that when stripped of everything external, the only wealth that mattered was what lived within. By that measure, she was only beginning to discover whether she was truly rich or desperately poor—and which of her companions possessed the resources that would truly matter in the days ahead.

CHAPTER SIX

New Hierarchies

E liza woke to the sound of rhythmic chopping, her body stiff from a night spent on the unyielding ground. For a disorienting moment, she struggled to reconcile her surroundings with her last conscious memories. The lean-to shelter, the palm fronds overhead, the absence of silk sheets—reality rushed back with jarring clarity.

They were stranded. The Aurora was gone. The carefully ordered world she had inhabited for years had dissolved overnight, replaced by this primitive existence where her designer wardrobe and social graces held no currency.

Beside her, Richard slept on, his face slack in unconsciousness, looking somehow diminished without his typical expression of confident authority. Eliza slipped quietly from the shelter, wincing as her muscles protested the sudden movement after hours of inactivity.

The morning sun bathed the beach in golden light, transforming their dire circumstances into a scene of incongruous beauty. White sand stretched in both directions, meeting turquoise water that sparkled innocently, as if it hadn't nearly claimed their lives hours earlier.

The chopping sound drew her attention to where Marco worked several yards from their shelter. He'd removed his shirt in the growing heat, revealing a torso sculpted by actual labor rather than carefully calibrated gym sessions. Lean muscle shifted beneath sun-darkened skin as he methodically cut palm fronds with a makeshift knife fashioned from debris.

He'd been busy while they slept. The original shelter had been reinforced and expanded, with a second lean-to structure taking shape nearby. A small fire smoldered near the entrance, suggesting he'd been up for hours.

Eliza approached quietly, suddenly conscious of her disheveled appearance. Her expensive resort wear, selected to flatter her figure on the yacht's deck, had been transformed by salt water and rough use. The silk blouse clung to her body in ways that would have been considered vulgar in her previous life, while tears along the seams revealed glimpses of skin she would normally have kept carefully hidden from anyone but Richard.

Marco looked up at her approach, his gaze quickly assessing before returning to his task. "Morning," he said simply. "Water's in the shell by the fire."

Eliza found the large conch shell he'd indicated, filled with fresh water. She drank gratefully, the simple pleasure more satisfying than any champagne she'd ever tasted aboard the Aurora.

"You've been busy," she observed, taking in the extent of his improvements to their situation.

Marco nodded, using the back of his forearm to wipe sweat from his brow. "Shelter's the priority today. We need better protection from the elements. Then water storage. Then sustainable food."

His methodical prioritization of their needs struck Eliza as both alien and compelling—a way of thinking she'd never needed to develop in her cushioned existence.

"How can I help?" she asked, the question emerging naturally despite its unfamiliarity on her lips.

Marco paused, studying her as if reassessing her capabilities. "Can you weave these palm fronds together?" He demonstrated a simple crosshatch pattern. "We need more coverage for the roof before the afternoon heat hits."

Eliza nodded, taking the fronds he offered. Her first attempts were clumsy, society hands struggling with work they'd never been trained to perform. Yet there was something oddly satisfying about the tangible nature of the task—unlike the ephemeral social maneuvering that had occupied her previous days, this effort produced visible, necessary results.

"Like this?" she asked after completing her first section.

Marco examined her work, his expression betraying mild surprise at her quick grasp of the technique. "Good. Keep going. We'll need about twenty sections that size."

They worked in companionable silence, the rhythm of their efforts creating a strange sense of partnership Eliza had rarely experienced. Aboard the yacht, their interactions had been governed by rigid hierarchy—client and service provider, each role carefully defined and maintained. Now, those artificial boundaries had dissolved, leaving only the fundamental assessment of what each could contribute to their survival.

"What the hell is going on?"

Richard's voice shattered the peaceful productivity of the morning. He stood at the shelter's entrance, hair disheveled, clothes wrinkled, face creased with sleep and dismay.

"You're building... huts?" The disbelief in his tone suggested he'd expected to wake to rescue, or at minimum, to a more civilized accommodation than what Marco had constructed.

"Improving our shelter," Marco corrected without pausing in his work. "We need better protection from sun and rain."

Richard limped toward them, wincing with each step on the unfamiliar terrain. "Where's breakfast? And for God's sake, is there coffee?"

Eliza exchanged a glance with Marco, reading in his carefully neutral expression the same assessment she'd reached: Richard still hadn't grasped the fundamental reality of their situation.

"Richard," she began carefully, "we don't have those things. We have what Marco has been able to gather or salvage."

"Then he should focus on finding proper food rather than playing Robinson Crusoe with palm leaves." Richard's tone carried the familiar note of executive authority that had served him well in boardrooms but seemed jarringly out of place on this deserted beach.

Marco set his knife down deliberately, rising to his full height with smooth, controlled motion. Even disheveled from their ordeal, he projected a physical authority that made Richard's corporate command seem hollow by comparison.

"Water, shelter, food, rescue—in that order," he stated, his voice level but firm. "Those are survival priorities. Not comfort, not convenience."

Richard bristled visibly, unused to having his dictates questioned, much less overruled. "I'm well aware of what's important. I'm saying we should focus on rescue and sustenance, not primitive construction projects."

"The emergency beacon is active," Marco replied. "Until help arrives—which could be days or weeks—we need to create sustainable living conditions."

"Days or weeks?" Richard's voice rose incredulously. "Do you have any idea who I am? There will be search parties already. My company alone has resources—"

"Your company doesn't know where to look," Marco interrupted, his patience visibly thinning. "We diverted from our course at your insistence, directly into the storm path. The yacht sank without getting off a precise mayday. The emergency beacon transmits our position, but with shipping lanes disrupted by the storm, detection could take time."

The stark assessment hung in the air between them. Eliza watched Richard's face as the reality of their situation finally penetrated his denial. For a moment, naked fear replaced his imperious expression, quickly masked by renewed bluster.

"This is completely unacceptable," he declared, as if their circumstances were a hotel suite that could be upgraded with a stern word to management.

"Richard," Eliza intervened, sensing the escalating tension between the men. "Marco knows what he's doing. We should follow his lead until rescue comes."

Her husband turned to her, genuinely shocked by what he clearly interpreted as betrayal. "Follow his lead? He works for us, Eliza. Or have you forgotten that along with your basic grooming?" His gaze flicked dismissively over her disheveled appearance, lingering on the torn sections of her blouse that revealed more skin than she'd intended.

Eliza felt heat rise to her cheeks—not embarrassment at her exposure, but anger at his casual contempt. Before she could respond, Marco spoke, his tone deliberately neutral but carrying undeniable authority.

"Employment contracts don't mean much here. Survival experience does." He gestured toward the shelter he'd constructed. "If you want to help, we need more fronds for the roof. If not, stay hydrated and out of the sun. Your choice."

Without waiting for Richard's response, he returned to his work, effectively dismissing the man who had been his employer twenty-four hours earlier. The power shift was so complete, so undeniable, that even Richard seemed momentarily stunned into silence.

Eliza returned to her weaving, acutely conscious of Richard's stunned expression. She'd never sided against him publicly in their marriage, had always played the role of supportive wife regardless of her private reservations. Yet here, stripped of social pretense, the choice between Richard's hollow authority and Marco's genuine capability seemed suddenly, blindingly clear.

"This is temporary," Richard finally said, his tone clipped. "When we're rescued, there will be consequences."

Marco didn't even look up. "Consequences come either way. My priority is keeping us alive until rescue arrives. Do what you want with that information."

Richard stalked away, radiating injured dignity despite his bedraggled appearance. Eliza watched him go, feeling a strange mixture of sympathy for his disorientation and frustration at his inability to adapt to their circumstances.

"He's struggling to accept our situation," she said softly, not quite an apology but an acknowledgment of the difficult dynamic.

Marco glanced at her, his expression softening fractionally. "Adaptation is hardest for those who've never had to bend." The observation carried no judgment, just understanding—as if he'd seen this pattern play out before in other disasters, other moments when reality stripped away pretense.

They returned to their work, but the morning's peaceful productivity had been replaced by an undercurrent of tension. Eliza was acutely aware of her position between the two men—legally bound to Richard through marriage, yet increasingly drawn to Marco's capable pragmatism. The traditional hierarchy dictated loyalty to her husband, yet survival demanded alignment with Marco's knowledge.

As the sun climbed higher, her torn blouse became increasingly problematic. Salt and sweat had rendered the expensive silk almost transparent in places, while the tears along the seams widened with each movement. Eliza caught Marco's gaze flickering toward her exposed skin several times, though he quickly averted his eyes with professional discipline.

The awareness of his notice sent an unexpected heat through her body that had nothing to do with the tropical sun. In her previous life, male appreciation of her appearance had been a tool, a currency she deployed strategically. Here, Marco's carefully controlled response to her inadvertent exposure felt different—more authentic, more potent for being restrained.

"I should find something else to wear," she said finally, the practical statement carrying undercurrents neither of them acknowledged.

Marco nodded, reaching for a bundle near the expanded shelter. "I found this washed ashore. Staff uniform shirt from the yacht. Not elegant, but sturdy."

He handed her a white cotton shirt, relatively intact despite its journey through the storm. The simple garment—designed for yacht crew rather than wealthy clients—represented another shift in their rapidly evolving circumstances.

"Thank you," Eliza said, genuinely grateful despite the garment's humble origins.

"There's a sheltered spot behind those palms," Marco indicated with a nod. "Private enough to change."

The consideration in his gesture touched her unexpectedly. Despite their dire situation and the necessary collapse of normal social boundaries, he maintained a respect for her dignity that felt more genuine than the performative deference he'd shown aboard the yacht.

Eliza retreated to the indicated spot, quickly exchanging her ruined silk blouse for the sturdy cotton shirt. The garment was too large, clearly intended for a male crew member, yet she found herself appreciating its practical comfort more than any designer piece in her extensive wardrobe. She rolled the sleeves to her elbows and knotted the excess material at her waist, creating a makeshift fit that felt strangely liberating in its practicality.

When she returned to the shelter construction, Marco's brief glance contained what might have been approval—not of her appearance, but of her practical adaptation. The simple acknowledgment felt more genuinely flattering than any compliment she'd received at Manhattan galas.

"I thought we might check the island for food sources," he said, securing the last section of the expanded shelter roof. "Basic foraging. Learn what's safe to eat."

"I'd like that," Eliza replied, surprising herself with her genuine interest. In her previous life, food had been primarily decorative and social—calorie-counted restaurant meals or catered events where consumption was secondary to appearance. The idea of food as necessary sustenance, something to be actively sought rather than passively selected from a menu, represented yet another fundamental shift in her reality.

Richard sat in the shade of the original shelter, watching their interaction with narrowed eyes. "And what am I supposed to do while you two play jungle explorer?" His tone carried accusation beneath the question.

"Rest and recover," Marco replied evenly. "You took the worst of the seasickness yesterday. Dehydration is still a risk. Drink water regularly."

The practical advice, delivered without condescension yet still positioning Richard as the weakest member of their group, clearly rankled. His mouth tightened, but before he could respond, Eliza intervened.

"We won't be gone long, Richard. Marco's right—you should rest today. We need you stronger for tomorrow."

Her diplomatic phrasing seemed to partially placate her husband, though his expression remained resentful as they prepared to depart. Eliza felt a twinge of guilt at the relief she experienced walking away from the camp with Marco, leaving Richard and his demands behind.

They moved inland along a narrow animal track, Marco pointing out landmarks to help orient her to their surroundings. The jungle closed around them quickly, creating a green cathedral of filtered light and unfamiliar sounds. In her previous life, Eliza would have found the environment threatening, possibly even terrifying. Now, guided by Marco's confident presence, she discovered an unexpected wonder in the island's wild beauty.

"Watch your step," Marco cautioned, his hand briefly touching the small of her back as he guided her around a treacherous root system. The contact, though fleeting and practical, sent an electric awareness through Eliza's body. She was suddenly, acutely conscious of their isolation—not just from civilization, but from witnessing eyes. Here in the island's interior, they existed beyond social judgment, beyond the rules and roles that had governed their interactions aboard the yacht.

The realization should have frightened her. Instead, it created a heady sensation of freedom, a lightness she couldn't remember experiencing since childhood.

"Here," Marco said, stopping beside a low-growing shrub covered in small red berries. "These are safe to eat. High in vitamin C. Good against scurvy." He plucked one, offering it to her with an open palm.

Eliza took the berry, her fingers brushing his calloused skin in a contact that lingered perhaps a moment longer than necessary.

She studied the fruit briefly before placing it in her mouth, the tart sweetness exploding on her tongue with an intensity that made her gasp softly.

"Good?" Marco asked, something like amusement warming his typically neutral expression.

"Amazing," she admitted. "I've never tasted anything like it."

"Wild foods often have stronger flavors than cultivated ones," he explained, moving behind her to reach more berries. The proximity brought his chest within inches of her back, his arm extending alongside hers to demonstrate which berries were ripest. "Look for the deep red ones, like this."

His voice came close to her ear, his breath stirring the loose strands of hair at her neck. Eliza felt her pulse quicken, her body responding to his nearness with an intensity that caught her off guard. This wasn't the calculated awareness she'd cultivated during society flirtations, but something more primal—a response to Marco as elemental man rather than social being.

"Like these?" she asked, reaching for a cluster he'd indicated, intensely conscious of how the movement brought her back into contact with his chest for a brief, electric moment.

"Perfect," he confirmed, his voice carrying a rougher edge than before. He stepped back slightly, creating distance between them, though Eliza could feel his gaze on her as she gathered more berries into a makeshift pouch she'd created from the lower hem of her borrowed shirt.

They continued deeper into the island's interior, Marco pointing out other edible plants—tubers that could be roasted, leaves that provided both nutrition and medicinal properties, fruits that would ripen in the coming weeks. With each discovery, he guided her hands with gentle precision, showing her how to identify, gather, and in some cases prepare what they found.

The education was practical, focused entirely on survival, yet Eliza couldn't ignore the sensual undercurrent of their interaction. Each time Marco's hands closed over hers to demonstrate proper technique, each instance where their bodies aligned as he showed her how to extract a particular root or reach a specific fruit, the awareness between them seemed to intensify.

"Your husband will be wondering where we are," Marco said finally, glancing at the sun's position. "We should head back."

The reminder of Richard's existence—and her marital status—landed like cold water on Eliza's heightened senses. Reality reasserted itself, the strange intimacy of their foraging expedition giving way to awareness of her actual circumstances. She was a married woman, temporarily stranded with her husband and a man who had been their employee just days earlier. Whatever she might be feeling was inappropriate, a product of stress and proximity rather than genuine connection.

Yet as they made their way back toward camp, their bodies moving in unexpected synchronization through the dense undergrowth, Eliza couldn't entirely convince herself of this rationalization. Something fundamental had shifted between them during their time alone in the jungle—an acknowledgment neither spoke aloud but both seemed to recognize.

They returned to find Richard exactly where they'd left him, though he'd moved his position to remain in the shade as the sun traveled overhead. His expression darkened as he took in their arrival, particularly the easy physicality that had developed between them during their expedition.

"Finally," he said, struggling to his feet. "I was beginning to think you'd abandoned me here."

The accusation, though delivered in his typical sardonic tone, carried genuine anxiety beneath the surface. For the first time, Eliza recognized what she hadn't allowed herself to see before: Richard was afraid. Beneath his demands and complaints lay the terror of a man whose entire identity had been built on control suddenly finding himself utterly powerless.

"We found food," she said gently, displaying their gathered provisions. "Berries, some tubers that Marco says we can roast, leaves for tea."

Richard glanced dismissively at their harvest. "Playing pre-historic gatherers. Charming. Meanwhile, I've been thinking about actual solutions to our situation. We need to improve the signal from that emergency beacon, perhaps build a fire large enough to be spotted from aircraft."

Marco set down his portion of their gathered food, his expression neutral but his body language expressing clear disagreement. "The beacon operates on frequencies specifically monitored by rescue services. A fire would be seen only if someone happened to be looking in this exact direction, which is unlikely given our location off established shipping and aircraft routes."

"So we just sit here eating berries and waiting to be discovered by accident?" Richard demanded, his voice rising with frustration. "That's your expert survival plan?"

"We survive until rescue comes," Marco replied evenly. "That means establishing sustainable food, water, and shelter. Not wasting energy on signal fires that have minimal chance of success."

"And who put you in charge of these decisions?" Richard's face flushed with anger. "Last I checked, you were employed to serve drinks on my yacht, not dictate survival strategy to your betters."

The crude reassertion of hierarchy hung in the air between them. Eliza watched Marco's expression, expecting anger or at least irritation at the deliberate humiliation. Instead, his face remained calm, almost detached, as if Richard's attempt to reestablish dominance was too transparently desperate to warrant emotional response.

"The situation has changed," Marco said simply. "Skills matter now, not titles or bank accounts. I'm doing what's necessary to keep us alive until rescue. You're welcome to contribute constructively or to go your own way."

"Go my own way?" Richard's voice rose incredulously. "On an island the size of Central Park? Don't be absurd."

"Then contribute," Marco suggested, his tone still infuriatingly reasonable. "Or at minimum, don't interfere with what needs to be done."

Richard turned to Eliza, clearly expecting her support in this power struggle. "Are you going to let him speak to me this way? To us? Have you forgotten who we are—who you are—just because we're temporarily inconvenienced?"

The appeal to their shared social identity struck Eliza as simultaneously compelling and hollow. She was Richard Harrington's wife, accustomed to the deference and privileges that position entailed. Yet standing on this beach, surrounded by the tangible results of Marco's knowledge and efforts—shelter that would protect them, food that would sustain them—the artificial nature of their previous hierarchy had never been more apparent.

"I think," she said carefully, "that Marco's experience is our best resource right now. We should respect that until rescue comes."

Richard stared at her as if she'd begun speaking in tongues. In all their years of marriage, Eliza had never openly contradicted him in front of others. Her role had been to support, to enhance, to reflect his importance rather than to challenge it. The shift in their dynamic seemed to disturb him more profoundly than any physical danger they faced.

"I see," he said finally, his voice cold. "Well, perhaps when we return to civilization, you might consider remaining here with your new tribal chief. You seem to have adapted remarkably quickly to primitive living."

The cruel suggestion was so unlike Richard's typically controlled public persona that Eliza knew it revealed genuine fear beneath his anger. Still, the words stung, highlighting the chasm growing between them with each hour on the island.

"Richard, that's not fair," she began, but Marco interrupted, his voice calm yet carrying unmistakable authority.

"Enough. This doesn't help anyone." He turned to collect the foraged food, effectively dismissing the argument. "We should prepare these roots before dark. They require cooking to be digestible."

The practical focus deflated the emotional tension, redirecting their energy toward the immediate necessities of survival. Richard retreated to the shelter, his rigid posture expressing continued resistance to their new reality, while Eliza moved to help Marco prepare their simple meal.

As they worked together, the easy rhythm of their cooperation provided stark contrast to the strained interaction with Richard. Marco showed her how to prepare the tubers, their hands occasionally brushing in the shared task, each contact sending a subtle current of awareness through Eliza's body.

"He's struggling to adjust," Marco observed quietly, nodding toward where Richard sat brooding in the shelter. "It's not unusual. People accustomed to power often have the hardest time adapting to situations where that power means nothing."

The insight revealed a depth of understanding Eliza hadn't expected. "You've seen this before?"

Marco nodded, his hands continuing their methodical work on the food. "In the military. In disaster zones. Status hierarchies collapse quickly when survival is at stake. Some people can't handle the leveling."

"And some adapt," Eliza suggested, thinking of her own surprising adjustment to their circumstances.

Marco glanced at her, something like approval warming his typically guarded expression. "Some discover strengths they never knew they had."

The simple observation, delivered without flattery or condescension, touched Eliza more deeply than any practiced compliment she'd received in her previous life. Marco saw her—not as Richard Harrington's beautiful wife or as a wealthy client to be served, but as a person revealing unexpected capabilities under pressure.

As the sun began its descent toward the horizon, they cooked the gathered roots in the small fire Marco had built, the simple meal taking on significance beyond mere sustenance. This was food they had gathered together, prepared with their own hands, untouched by the elaborate artifice of restaurant presentation or social performance.

Richard eventually emerged to accept his portion, hunger overcoming pride, though he ate in silence, physically present but emotionally separated from their small community. The unresolved tension cast a shadow over the evening, creating

three distinct islands of experience despite their physical proximity.

Night fell quickly in the tropics, darkness spreading across
the beach like spilled ink. Marco built up the fire to ward off the
evening chill, the flames casting flickering shadows across their
faces, highlighting the transformation each had undergone in
the brief time since the yacht's sinking.

"We should conserve the flashlight battery," Marco said,
checking the small device from his emergency pouch. "Fire for
light when necessary, otherwise adapt to the natural rhythms of
daylight and darkness."

"Like animals," Richard muttered, his first words in hours.

"Like humans did for thousands of years before electricity,"
Marco corrected mildly. "Our bodies are designed for it, even if
we've forgotten."

The simple observation carried philosophical weight that
hung in the air between them. They had been stripped of the
technological buffer that separated modern humans from natural rhythms, forced back into patterns their distant ancestors
would have recognized.

As they prepared for another night in the shelter, the forced
intimacy of their sleeping arrangement created renewed tension. The structure Marco had expanded would protect them
from elements but required close physical proximity—a necessity that carried different implications for each of them.

Richard positioned himself as far from Marco as the confined space allowed, turning his back in silent protest against

their circumstances. Eliza found herself once again caught in the middle—socially bound to her husband yet increasingly drawn to the quiet strength Marco embodied.

She lay awake long after the others had fallen silent, listening to the unfamiliar symphony of island night sounds. The man she had married and the man who had once served them drinks now slept within arm's reach of each other, their previous social distance collapsed by necessity into uncomfortable intimacy.

In the darkness, stripped of visual cues, Eliza became acutely aware of the men's distinct presences—Richard's restless, resentful energy even in sleep, and Marco's contained, watchful calm. Though no words had been spoken, no lines crossed, she recognized the dangerous current developing between herself and the former crewman.

Beyond physical attraction, beyond the obvious competence gap between the men, something more fundamental was emerging: the recognition that the qualities she had valued in her previous life—wealth, status, social position—had been revealed as hollow currency in this new reality. What mattered now was capability, adaptability, and a kind of authentic strength she had never before considered essential.

As sleep finally began to claim her, Eliza faced the disquieting realization that the island wasn't just stripping away physical comforts—it was systematically dismantling the very foundations of identity she had built her life upon. And in that dismantling lay both terror and an unexpected, forbidden exhilaration.

CHAPTER SEVEN

Adapting

D ays blended into each other with surprising speed, the rhythm of survival replacing the structured calendar that had previously governed Eliza's existence. Sunrise to sunset, their lives now revolved around fundamental necessities—water, food, shelter, safety. The luxury yacht and Manhattan penthouse might as well have existed in another lifetime, so distant did they seem from this new reality.

A week into their island existence, the transformation in their small encampment was remarkable. Marco's initial lean-to shelter had evolved into a surprisingly sophisticated structure, with separate sleeping areas, a covered cooking space, and even rudimentary furniture fashioned from salvaged yacht debris and island materials. Each morning brought new improvements—a rack for drying clothing, a stone-lined pit for more controlled cooking fires, containers woven from palm fronds to store their gathered food.

Eliza found herself fully engaged in this primitive domestic-ity, her hands growing calloused from work that would have been unimaginable in her previous life. She developed routines with Marco that required no verbal coordination—rising at dawn to collect fresh water, gathering fruits from nearby trees, weaving additional palm fronds for ongoing shelter improve-ments. Their bodies moved in unconscious synchronization, anticipating each other's needs with a wordless understanding that grew more fluid with each passing day.

Richard remained a reluctant participant in their survival community. He accepted the benefits of their labor—eating the food they gathered, sleeping in the shelter they built—while contributing minimal effort to its creation. His initial denial had given way to a sullen acceptance of their circumstances, though he maintained the fiction that rescue was imminent, refusing to fully commit to the work of long-term survival.

"The signal from the emergency beacon is strong," he repeat-ed each morning, checking the device Marco had salvaged from the raft. "They'll find us any day now."

Marco neither confirmed nor denied these assertions, focus-ing instead on the practical realities of their situation. "The water catchment system needs reinforcement," he would say, or "We should smoke some of the fish today for longer storage." His priorities remained resolutely immediate—what needed to be done to ensure another day of survival, regardless of whether rescue came tomorrow or months from now.

This morning found Eliza and Marco expanding their food storage area, using palm fronds she had woven into surprisingly sturdy baskets. The sun beat down on her shoulders, now tanned to a deep honey gold that matched the streaks lightening her once-carefully maintained hair. Her body had changed in subtle but significant ways—leaner from the combination of physical labor and simpler diet, yet somehow stronger than she'd ever been despite regular sessions with Manhattan's most exclusive trainers.

"These should hold the tubers," she said, displaying her latest baskets with quiet pride.

Marco nodded approval, his own physical transformation even more pronounced. His already athletic frame had grown more defined, muscles hardened by constant labor, skin darkened to a deep bronze by daily exposure to the tropical sun. He'd fashioned a makeshift knife from salvaged metal and wore it in a sheath at his waist—a primitive accessory that nevertheless struck Eliza as perfectly suited to the elemental masculinity he embodied.

"Good work," he acknowledged, examining her baskets with genuine appreciation. "Your weaving's getting tight enough to hold water soon."

The simple compliment warmed her more than any elaborate flattery she'd received in her previous life. Marco's approval carried weight precisely because it was earned rather than automatically granted due to her appearance or social position.

Richard emerged from the sleeping shelter, his transformation less harmonious than theirs. Though physically changed by their island existence—thinner, somewhat tanned, his designer stubble now a patchy beard—he carried himself with the air of a man temporarily inconvenienced rather than fundamentally altered. His eyes narrowed at their easy companionship.

"Playing house again?" he observed acidly. "How domestic."

Eliza had grown accustomed to these barbs, recognizing them as expressions of helplessness rather than genuine cruelty. Richard's entire identity had been built around a social and financial power that meant nothing in their current circumstances. His inability to contribute meaningfully left him only bitter commentary as a means of asserting presence.

"We're improving food storage," she replied evenly. "There are berries ripening in the eastern grove if you'd like to help gather them."

"I'll pass," he said dismissively. "Someone needs to maintain the emergency beacon and monitor for rescue signals."

The beacon required no maintenance, as they all knew, but the fiction gave Richard purpose and spared them his ineffectual attempts at physical labor. Eliza exchanged a glance with Marco, reading in his eyes the same assessment—better to let Richard believe he contributed than force the issue.

As Richard wandered toward the beach, ostensibly to "scan the horizon" for rescue vessels, Marco turned back to their work.

"I've been thinking about protein sources. The fish in the lagoon are plentiful, but we need better tools than improvised spears."

"What do you have in mind?" Eliza asked, finding herself genuinely interested in survival strategies that would have seemed absurdly primitive weeks earlier.

"Traps," Marco replied, already gathering materials. "I'll show you."

The casual "I'll show you" had become a recurring theme in their relationship—Marco sharing knowledge accumulated through years of training and experience, Eliza absorbing it with surprising aptitude. Each lesson diminished the distance between them, creating a partnership based on shared capability rather than artificial social roles.

Her borrowed crew shirt, once oversized and crisp, had deteriorated to little more than a frayed covering. The sleeves had been torn away for use as bindings for shelter components, leaving her arms fully exposed to the sun. The hem had gradually shortened as she'd sacrificed strips of fabric for various survival needs, now barely reaching mid-thigh. Combined with her abbreviated shorts, also showing signs of extreme wear, her appearance would have been considered scandalously revealing in her previous life.

Here, such concerns seemed absurdly trivial. Practicality governed everything, including clothing. Yet Eliza occasionally caught Marco's gaze lingering on the exposed length of her legs or the curve of her shoulder revealed by the widening tears in her shirt—moments of masculine appreciation quickly controlled but undeniably present.

The awareness of his notice sent unexpected heat through her body, a response she justified as natural human reaction to isolation and proximity. Yet in honest moments, usually in the darkness before sleep claimed her, Eliza acknowledged a deeper truth: her attraction to Marco had little to do with circumstance and everything to do with the man himself—his quiet competence, his uncompromising authenticity, his respect for her emerging capabilities.

These thoughts remained carefully unexamined in daylight hours as they moved through their survival routines with practical focus. Today's lesson in fish trapping led them to the shallow waters of the lagoon, where Marco demonstrated how to weave flexible branches into funnel-shaped devices that would guide fish in but prevent their escape.

"The principle is simple," he explained, his hands moving with practiced precision. "Fish swim forward instinctively when seeking escape. The narrowing passage makes return impossible."

Eliza worked alongside him, attempting to replicate his technique, acutely aware of his proximity as he occasionally reached over to correct her weaving. Each guidance brought his body briefly against hers, his hands closing over her fingers to demonstrate proper placement—contact that sent awareness shimmering across her skin despite the practicality of its purpose.

"Like this?" she asked, holding up her nearly completed trap.

Marco examined it with genuine assessment rather than automatic approval. "The entrance needs to be wider, but the weave is good. They'll definitely work."

The genuine pleasure Eliza felt at his approval surprised her. In her previous life, success had been measured in social currency—the envy of other wives, the approval of Richard's business associates, the perfect execution of expected appearances. Here, success was tangible and immediate—a trap that would actually function, providing food they genuinely needed.

They waded into the lagoon's shallows to place their traps, the warm water swirling around Eliza's thighs, further dampening her already abbreviated clothing. Marco moved with the easy grace that characterized all his actions, his body seeming perfectly adapted to this environment despite its stark difference from the naval vessels and luxury yachts of his previous experience.

"We'll check them tomorrow morning," he said as they secured the last trap. "Dawn is usually best for harvest."

As they turned to wade back to shore, movement near the beach caught their attention. Richard stood at the water's edge, a crudely fashioned spear in his hands, his expression set in determined lines.

"What's he doing?" Eliza asked quietly.

Marco assessed the situation with a single glance. "Trying to prove something," he replied, his tone neutral but carrying undercurrents of concern.

They watched as Richard waded awkwardly into the shallows, spear raised in an approximation of the stance he'd observed Marco use days earlier. His movements lacked the fluid economy that characterized Marco's hunting, his body tense with effort rather than relaxed with practiced skill.

"Should we help him?" Eliza asked, recognizing the potential for both injury and humiliation in Richard's clumsy attempt.

Marco considered briefly. "Sometimes people need to learn their own lessons," he said finally. "But we'll stay close."

They remained in the lagoon, continuing to adjust their traps while keeping Richard in peripheral vision. His first attempts at spearing fish were predictably unsuccessful—lunging too soon, moving too suddenly, failing to account for water's refraction effect on visible targets.

After twenty minutes of increasing frustration, Richard finally spotted a larger fish hovering near a coral outcropping. With a shout of triumph, he plunged the spear downward with all his strength—and promptly lost his footing on the slippery lagoon bottom. He crashed forward into the water, the spear embedding itself in the sandy bottom as he flailed and sputtered.

Marco was moving before Eliza fully registered what had happened, reaching Richard in powerful strokes as the other man struggled to regain his footing. The seafloor dropped away sharply beyond the coral, creating a sudden depth that had caught Richard unprepared.

"I've got you," Marco said calmly, his arm circling Richard's chest with professional efficiency, supporting him as they moved back toward shallower water.

Richard's face flushed with humiliation as his feet found purchase on the lagoon floor again. He shook off Marco's supporting arm with angry force.

"I didn't need rescue," he snapped. "I was perfectly fine."

"Of course," Marco agreed smoothly, stepping back to give Richard space to recover his dignity. "The drop-off can surprise anyone their first time hunting this area."

The reasonable tone only seemed to inflame Richard's embarrassment. "I don't need your condescension," he snarled, struggling toward shore with wounded pride practically radiating from his stiff posture.

Eliza moved to follow, but Marco's light touch on her arm stopped her. "Let him go," he advised quietly. "Pride heals better in private."

She nodded, understanding the wisdom in his suggestion. Richard's sense of inadequacy was painfully apparent, his failed attempt at proving himself only highlighting the capabilities gap between the men. No words of comfort would mitigate that reality.

They finished securing the traps in silence, giving Richard time to retreat to the shelter and compose himself. By the time they returned to camp, he had positioned himself at the far edge of their clearing, methodically checking the emergency beacon yet again—retreating to the one task he had claimed as his domain.

The remainder of the afternoon passed in this uneasy configuration—Marco and Eliza continuing their survival work with seamless coordination while Richard maintained deliberate distance, his earlier humiliation creating a palpable barrier between them.

As sunset approached, the familiar ritual of fire-building and meal preparation temporarily bridged their divided community. Whatever tensions existed during daylight hours, the primal comfort of gathered food and warming flames created a tentative connection that transcended personal conflicts.

Their evening meal consisted of fruits harvested that morning, roots Marco had shown Eliza how to identify and prepare, and the last portions of a fish he'd speared the previous day. Simple fare by civilized standards, yet Eliza found herself appreciating the direct connection between effort and sustenance—so different from restaurant meals ordered with detached entitlement.

As darkness settled fully around them, stars emerging in breathtaking profusion overhead, the evening fire cast flickering shadows across their faces. These night hours had developed their own rhythm—a time for reflection and conversation that daytime's constant demands didn't permit.

"Do you think they're still searching?" Richard asked suddenly, breaking the extended silence. The question lacked his usual defensive edge, revealing genuine vulnerability instead.

Marco considered before answering, his expression thought-ful in the firelight. "Standard search protocols run two weeks for missing vessels," he said honestly. "But your status might extend that. Companies with your resources often continue private searches beyond official timeframes."

The assessment was neither falsely optimistic nor unneces-sarily pessimistic—just another example of Marco's unflinching pragmatism. Eliza found herself appreciating this quality more with each passing day—his ability to face reality without either sugar-coating or catastrophizing it.

"My board won't give up easily," Richard asserted, though his tone lacked its usual confidence. "Too much institutional knowledge at stake."

The phrasing struck Eliza as revealing—not "They won't give up on me" but "Too much institutional knowledge at stake." Even in contemplating his own rescue, Richard defined his val-ue in terms of business utility rather than human connection.

A contemplative silence settled around them, broken only by the crackling of the fire and distant ocean sounds. These evening hours had gradually evolved into a time of unexpected sharing, perhaps facilitated by darkness that obscured facial expressions and fire-glow that softened hard realities.

"How did you end up on luxury yachts?" Eliza asked Marco, the question emerging from genuine curiosity rather than social formality. "After naval special forces, it seems..."

"A step down?" Marco finished wryly when she hesitated.

"Different," she amended diplomatically.

Marco prodded the fire with a stick, sending sparks spiraling upward into the night sky. For a moment, Eliza thought he might deflect the question, maintaining the professional distance he'd cultivated even as their circumstances collapsed other boundaries between them.

"I needed..." he began, then paused, reconsidering. "After my last deployment, I wanted simplicity. Clear expectations, defined parameters. The ocean without combat scenarios."

The glimpse into his motivation revealed more than the facts of his transition. Eliza found herself wondering about those deployments, what experiences had driven this capable, confident man to seek refuge in service roles beneath his obvious capabilities.

"You could have commanded your own vessel," she observed. "With your qualifications."

Marco shrugged, the firelight highlighting the fluid movement of muscle beneath his skin. "Command comes with responsibilities I wasn't interested in carrying anymore."

Richard snorted softly. "So you chose subservience instead? Fetching drinks for the wealthy? Hardly seems like a fair trade."

The deliberate provocation hung in the air between them. Eliza tensed, expecting Marco to respond with justified anger to the deliberate diminishment of his choices. Instead, he answered with unexpected openness.

"I chose freedom," he said simply. "Temporary contracts, different waters, no permanent attachments or long-term obligations. After years of duty that demanded everything, including parts of myself I wasn't prepared to lose, it felt like liberation."

The honesty of his response silenced even Richard's reflexive condescension. Eliza found herself reassessing Marco yet again—recognizing that his service role had been a conscious choice rather than a limitation, a deliberate stepping away from power rather than an inability to claim it.

"And now?" she asked quietly. "Stranded here with responsibility for our survival?"

Marco's gaze met hers across the fire, something like rueful acknowledgment in his expression. "Ironic, isn't it? But different. This is immediate—keeping us alive today, tomorrow. Not strategic decisions affecting hundreds of lives over months or years."

The distinction revealed a philosophy Eliza had never considered—different types of responsibility, different weights of command. Richard's business authority suddenly seemed simultaneously larger in scope yet smaller in immediate consequence than the leadership Marco now exercised in their daily survival.

Richard stood abruptly, clearly uncomfortable with the direction of conversation. "This servant talk is fascinating, but I think I'll turn in," he announced, the deliberate choice of words reasserting the social hierarchy he couldn't seem to relinquish despite its increasing irrelevance.

As he retreated to the sleeping shelter, Eliza felt a familiar mixture of embarrassment at his rudeness and resignation to its predictability. "I'm sorry," she said softly once Richard was beyond earshot. "He's struggling with..."

"Loss of identity," Marco finished when she trailed off. "It's not unusual. We define ourselves by what we do, what we control. When that's stripped away, some people can't adapt."

"And some can," Eliza observed, thinking of her own surprising adjustment to their circumstances.

Marco studied her across the dying fire, his gaze carrying an assessment that felt more genuinely appreciative than any flattery she'd received in her previous life. "You certainly have."

The simple observation, delivered without condescension or false praise, touched something deep within Eliza. In her marriage to Richard, her value had been primarily decorative—beauty to be displayed, charm to be deployed in service of his social and business objectives. Here, under Marco's guidance, she was becoming someone she'd never imagined possible—capable, resilient, genuinely useful.

"I should check the eastern perimeter before turning in," Marco said, rising from his position by the fire. "The wild pigs have been rooting near the fruit trees again."

Eliza nodded, watching his silhouette disappear into the darkness beyond their camp's perimeter. With both men absent, she found herself suddenly, acutely aware of the opportunity their temporary privacy provided.

After a week on the island, the lack of proper bathing facilities had become increasingly problematic. They'd managed basic cleanliness using freshwater from the inland stream, but the cramped, public nature of their camp offered no opportunity for the kind of thorough bathing her body increasingly craved.

The small lagoon where they'd placed fish traps that afternoon suddenly presented itself as a perfect solution—sheltered, private, and most importantly, currently deserted. The moon had risen fully now, casting sufficient light to navigate the short path from their camp to the water's edge. Richard was unlikely to reemerge from the shelter given his current mood, and Marco's perimeter check would take at least twenty minutes based on previous routines.

Decision made, Eliza gathered a small bundle containing a piece of fabric she'd been saving for use as a towel and a fragment of soap carefully rationed from Marco's emergency supplies. The opportunity for genuine cleanliness was too precious to ignore, worth the minor risk of nocturnal wildlife encounters between camp and lagoon.

The short walk through the moonlight awakened all her senses—the whisper of night breezes through palm fronds, the occasional calls of unfamiliar birds, the rich scents of vegetation and salt air mingling in the humid darkness. In her previous life, Eliza would have found such an excursion terrifying—wild nature experienced without protective barriers of civilization. Now, after a week of island existence, she moved with surprising confidence through the unfamiliar terrain.

The lagoon appeared before her like something from a travel brochure's fantasy—moonlight silvering its surface, gentle waves lapping at a crescent of white sand, palm trees creating theatrical silhouettes against the star-filled sky. The beauty stopped Eliza momentarily, its perfection somehow more affecting for being witnessed alone, without the mediating presence of cameras or social performance.

After checking the surrounding area for signs of wildlife or human presence, she set her small bundle on a flat rock near the water's edge. A moment's hesitation preceded the removal of her clothes—the ingrained modesty of civilized existence briefly asserting itself before surrendering to practical necessity.

The borrowed crew shirt and abbreviated shorts joined her towel on the rock, leaving Eliza completely naked beneath the tropical night sky. The sensation was simultaneously vulnerable and strangely liberating—her body fully exposed to the elements yet free from the constant assessment that had characterized her previous existence.

She waded into the lagoon, the warm water rising gradually along her legs, then hips, then torso as she moved deeper. The sensation was exquisite—the gentle pressure of water against skin that had known only air and rough fabric for days, the weightless support as she pushed off from the sandy bottom to float on her back beneath the vast blanket of stars overhead.

For several minutes, Eliza simply existed in this perfect moment—body suspended between sea and sky, mind emptied of concerns both immediate and distant. The woman floating in moonlit water seemed disconnected from both the socialite she'd been weeks earlier and the survivor she was becoming—existing temporarily in a liminal space between identities.

Eventually, practical concerns reasserted themselves. She moved to shallower water where she could stand comfortably, using the precious fragment of soap to create lather in her hands. The simple pleasure of cleansing her skin felt like extraordinary luxury after days of makeshift hygiene, each stroke of soapy hands across shoulders, breasts, abdomen removing not just physical grime but some intangible residue of her former self.

Her hair proved more challenging, the once-pampered strands now a salt-stiffened tangle that resisted her fingers' attempts at order. She ducked beneath the surface repeatedly, using water and the last of the soap to create some semblance of cleanliness if not the silken perfection her regular stylist had once achieved.

Lost in the sensory experience of her improvised bath, Eliza failed to notice the subtle shift in the jungle sounds behind her—the momentary silence of nocturnal creatures signaling human presence. It was only as she stood again in waist-deep water, arms raised to wring moisture from her hair, that some primal awareness alerted her to observation.

She turned sharply toward shore, arms instinctively crossing over her breasts in belated modesty. For a heart-stopping moment, she saw nothing—just moonlit beach and shadowed vegetation. Then movement caught her eye—a darker silhouette among the palms, the outline of broad shoulders and height that could only belong to Marco.

The moment stretched between them—Eliza frozen in sudden awareness of her nakedness, Marco motionless at the jungle's edge. Even across the distance separating them, she could feel the intensity of his gaze, the masculine appreciation he typically kept carefully controlled now unleashed by her unexpected vulnerability.

Before she could speak—though what words would have been appropriate, she couldn't imagine—Marco stepped backward into deeper shadow. His voice carried across the water, controlled but carrying undercurrents she'd never heard before.

"I'm sorry. I was checking the perimeter. I'll go."

The apology was genuine, his retreat immediate—no lingering gaze, no attempt to prolong the moment of her exposure. Yet the knowledge that he had seen her—truly seen her, without the barrier of clothing or social performance—sent heat flooding through Eliza's body that had nothing to do with the warm lagoon waters.

She remained motionless until certain of his departure, conflicting emotions washing through her with bewildering intensity. Embarrassment at being caught in such vulnerability warred with a more disturbing recognition—that part of her had responded to his gaze with something dangerously close to pleasure.

In her marriage to Richard, her body had been primarily transactional—beauty maintained through rigorous discipline, displayed to enhance his status, offered physically to secure her position. Being seen by Marco felt fundamentally different—his appreciation untainted by ownership, his desire evident yet controlled by respect.

Eliza completed her bathing in distracted haste, the sensual pleasure of moments earlier replaced by complicated awareness of boundaries crossed. She dried herself with the makeshift towel and donned her worn clothing, suddenly conscious of how little the tattered garments actually concealed.

The walk back to camp seemed longer, her senses hyper-alert for sounds of Marco's presence though logic told her he would have returned by a different route to avoid further awkwardness. The camp appeared undisturbed when she arrived, the fire burned to embers, the sleeping shelter quiet save for Richard's soft snoring from his curtained section.

Marco's sleeping area showed no sign of recent occupation, confirming her suspicion that he had deliberately delayed his return to camp, giving her time to settle without confrontation. The consideration in this choice—prioritizing her comfort over any attempt to address or exploit the vulnerable moment at the lagoon—touched Eliza unexpectedly.

She slipped into her own sleeping space, body clean but mind turbulent with unexamined implications. The simple fact remained—Marco had seen her naked in the moonlight, and something fundamental had shifted between them in that moment of unintended intimacy.

As sleep gradually claimed her, Eliza found herself wondering not about the propriety of what had happened, but about the expression she'd glimpsed on Marco's face in that brief moment of discovery—a complex mixture of desire, appreciation, and something that looked surprisingly like reverence.

Whatever was developing between them—and she could no longer deny something was—it bore no resemblance to the calculated transactions that had characterized her previous relationships with men. Here, stripped of wealth and status, reduced to most basic elements of human interaction, authentic connection had emerged in unexpected, potentially dangerous forms.

Tomorrow would require facing Marco with this new awareness between them, navigating the unspoken current that had been building since the yacht's sinking and now flowed too strongly to ignore. The proper response—retreat behind marriage vows and social conventions—competed with a more disturbing impulse toward exploration of these forbidden feelings.

Her last conscious thought before dreams claimed her was simple yet profound: the island wasn't just transforming her external circumstances or physical capabilities—it was revealing aspects of herself she'd never been permitted to acknowledge in the carefully constructed prison of her previous existence.

Freedom, she was discovering, carried both exhilaration and terror in equal measure.

CHAPTER EIGHT

Primal Awakening

Two weeks into their island existence, the provisional had become routine, the extraordinary transformed into daily reality. Their camp had evolved from desperate survival arrangement to functional living space, with systems for water collection, food preservation, and even basic comfort now established. What had been shocking deprivation in those first chaotic days after the shipwreck now felt strangely normal—a new standard of existence that required neither explanation nor apology.

Dawn found Eliza already at work, checking the fish traps she'd helped Marco set the previous evening. Her movements had acquired a confidence unimaginable in her previous life, her once-manicured hands now capable and calloused, moving with practiced efficiency as she extracted the night's catch from woven branches. The former socialite who had never prepared her own meals now cleaned fish with deft precision, preserving every usable part with a resourcefulness that would have horrified her Manhattan friends.

The thought brought an unexpected smile to her lips—not the practiced expression she'd perfected for society photographs, but something genuine that reached her eyes and transformed her face. There was satisfaction in this work, a tangible connection between effort and result that her decorative role in Richard's world had never provided.

From across the camp clearing, Marco observed her quiet pleasure, his own expression softening briefly before he returned to reinforcing their main shelter. The two weeks of shared survival had created a wordless understanding between them, a partnership that required minimal verbal coordination. They anticipated each other's movements, handed tools or materials at precisely the right moment, their bodies moving in unconscious synchronization through the rhythms of island life.

The night at the lagoon remained unmentioned between them, though its impact lingered in heightened awareness whenever proximity brought them into contact. Marco had maintained scrupulous respect for boundaries since that moment of unintended intimacy, yet Eliza felt his gaze following her movements with undisguised appreciation when he thought himself unobserved.

"Another successful hunt," she called, holding up the morning's catch—three substantial fish that would provide their main protein for the day.

Marco nodded approval, genuine respect in his assessment. "Your trap placement is getting better. You have good instincts for where they'll feed."

The simple acknowledgment of her developing skills warmed Eliza in ways that elaborate compliments about her appearance never had. Here, value was measured in contribution rather than ornamentation, and she found herself thriving under this new metric of worth.

Richard emerged from his separated sleeping area, beard now unkempt, hair lank despite the bathing opportunities Marco had created near their freshwater source. Unlike Eliza and Marco, whose physical transformations had taken on a honed, purposeful quality, Richard's changes suggested deterioration rather than adaptation. He had surrendered minimal effort to survival necessities but resisted the deeper adjustment to their circumstances, maintaining the fiction that rescue was imminent even as weeks stretched before them.

"Is there coffee?" he asked for perhaps the hundredth time, the habitual question less a genuine inquiry than a protest against their circumstances.

"Fresh water by the fire," Eliza replied evenly, having learned that engagement with his complaints only prolonged their expression. "And some fruit Marco gathered yesterday."

Richard's expression soured at the familiar response, his gaze darting between Marco's capable industry and Eliza's quiet competence with poorly disguised resentment. The island had revealed a fundamental truth about their marriage that civilization had allowed them to ignore—Richard's primary value had been financial provision, a currency that meant nothing in their current reality.

"I'll check the emergency beacon," he announced, retreating to the one task he had claimed as his domain, though they all knew the device required no maintenance.

Eliza exchanged a glance with Marco, a moment of silent understanding passing between them. They had evolved a tacit agreement regarding Richard—allowing him the fiction of contribution while the actual work of survival continued around him. Whether kindness or cowardice motivated this accommodation, neither could have articulated with certainty.

The morning progressed in its established rhythm—food preparation, water collection, ongoing improvements to their shelter and storage areas. Eliza found herself humming softly as she worked, a habit she'd developed in recent days that would have seemed ludicrously inappropriate in their dire circumstances just weeks earlier. Yet there was something undeniably satisfying in this simplified existence—immediate problems with clear solutions, tangible results from direct effort, freedom from the constant performance her previous life had required.

"I'm going to check the eastern fruit grove," she announced as midday approached. "The berries should be ripe by now."

Marco looked up from where he was fashioning a new knife from salvaged metal. "Take the walking stick. The ground's still soft from yesterday's rain."

His concern carried no hint of condescension, just practical assessment of conditions and risks. Eliza nodded, retrieving the sturdy branch he'd shaped for her use on uneven terrain. Such exchanges had become their normal—communication focused on genuine welfare rather than social formality.

"Back before evening," she promised, slinging the woven gathering basket across her body.

"Be careful," Marco added, his tone casual but his eyes conveying deeper meaning. They'd established reasonable safety protocols for solo excursions, but the island held unpredictable elements that demanded respect.

The path to the eastern grove had become familiar through repeated travel, though Eliza remained alert to her surroundings as Marco had taught her. Two weeks of island existence had transformed her relationship with the natural world—no longer did she view it with tourist appreciation or fearful distance, but as an environment to be read and understood, filled with both resources and hazards requiring equal acknowledgment.

The grove itself was a small paradise of fruit-bearing plants, some familiar from civilized markets, others unique to this tropical ecosystem. Marco had painstakingly taught her which were safe, which required special preparation, which to avoid entirely. Eliza moved through the dense greenery with practiced confidence, selecting the ripest specimens with discerning eye.

So absorbed was she in the gathering that the sudden rustling from nearby undergrowth didn't immediately register as unusual. By the time she identified the sound as larger than the small animals typically encountered, the wild boar had already emerged into the small clearing—bristled, tusked, and startlingly massive at close range.

Eliza froze, the basket of fruit suddenly forgotten in her hand. Marco had mentioned these creatures during his island orientation, emphasizing their unpredictable aggression and surprising speed. Adult males could weigh hundreds of pounds, their tusks capable of inflicting devastating wounds. The specimen regarding her with small, suspicious eyes easily matched that threatening description.

Time seemed to suspend as prey instinct warred with rational thought. Run? Remain motionless? Attempt intimidation? Every option carried potentially fatal consequences if incorrectly chosen.

The decision was made for her when the boar lowered its head slightly, a preliminary movement Marco had described as preceding a charge. Terror locked Eliza's limbs even as her mind screamed for action, the primitive brain recognizing mortal danger while the body remained paralyzed by fear.

The impact she anticipated never came. Instead, a blur of motion intercepted her vision as Marco materialized from the jungle's edge, positioning himself between Eliza and the advancing boar with a spear she hadn't known he carried. His stance was perfectly balanced, body coiled with controlled power as he faced the animal without visible fear.

The confrontation lasted mere seconds—Marco's aggressive advance and confident shout causing the boar to reconsider its attack. With a grunt of frustration, the animal veered sideways and crashed back into the undergrowth, leaving only trampled vegetation as evidence of the near-disaster.

Reaction hit Eliza like a physical blow, her legs buckling as adrenaline flooded her system. Marco's arm circled her waist before she could collapse, his body solid and reassuring against hers.

"It's okay," he murmured, his voice steady despite the elevated rhythm of his breathing. "You're safe."

The simple statement broke the paralysis that had gripped her, releasing a tremor that ran through her entire body. "I froze," she whispered, horror at her helplessness overwhelming relief at her escape. "I knew what to do but I couldn't—"

"Fear response is normal," Marco interrupted gently, his arm still supporting her weight. "Fight, flight, or freeze—none of us knows which our body will choose until the moment arrives."

The matter-of-fact assessment offered neither condemnation nor false comfort, just acknowledgment of human reality. Eliza found herself leaning into his strength, accepting support without the self-consciousness that would have colored such vulnerability in her previous life.

"How did you know?" she asked, gradually regaining steadiness in her limbs.

"I followed at a distance," Marco admitted, his expression suggesting he expected criticism for this revelation. "You've been going farther alone each day. It seemed prudent to maintain awareness of your location."

Rather than resenting the tacit supervision, Eliza felt unexpected warmth at his protective concern. In her marriage to Richard, she had been a possession to be displayed and maintained; Marco's protection stemmed from recognition of her value as a person, not an asset.

"Thank you," she said simply, the words encompassing more than gratitude for immediate rescue.

As the initial shock faded, Eliza became acutely aware of their physical proximity—Marco's arm still circling her waist, her body pressed against the solid warmth of his chest. The contact sparked awareness that transcended mere appreciation for safety, reminding her with jarring clarity of the growing attraction she'd been careful not to examine too closely.

"You're bleeding," Marco observed, gently turning her arm to reveal a long scratch she hadn't registered in the moment of danger. "Must have caught on thorns when you backed away."

The injury was minor—a surface abrasion that barely broke the skin—yet Marco studied it with focused concern. "We should clean this. Infection is the real danger here."

He guided her to a nearby fallen log, retrieving a small container of fresh water he carried for emergencies. With methodical gentleness, he cleansed the wound, his fingers moving with delicate precision despite their strength and calluses.

"This might sting," he warned, producing a small leaf she recognized from his previous medicinal teachings. When crushed, it released antiseptic properties that had served as their island pharmacy for minor injuries.

Eliza winced slightly as he applied the natural remedy, but found herself more distracted by the sensation of his hands on her skin than by the momentary discomfort. Marco worked with complete focus, apparently unaware of how his touch sent awareness shimmering through her body—or perhaps maintaining deliberate professional detachment despite similar recognition.

"There," he said finally, securing the leaf in place with a strip of clean cloth from his pocket. "Keep it covered until tomorrow. We'll check for signs of infection then."

His fingers lingered on her arm a moment longer than medical necessity required, the touch feather-light but resonating through Eliza's heightened senses. When she raised her eyes to his, the gratitude she intended to express died unspoken as she recognized the carefully controlled desire in his gaze—a hunger he had maintained behind disciplined restraint since their first meeting, now momentarily visible in the aftermath of danger and adrenaline.

The moment extended between them, possibility hanging in the humid air with almost tangible presence. Then, as if remembering himself, Marco withdrew his hand and rose from their shared seat on the log.

"We should head back," he said, voice roughened slightly despite his resumed composure. "Storm clouds building to the west."

Indeed, the quality of light had changed during their encounter, the previously clear sky now darkening with approaching weather. Tropical storms developed with startling speed on the island, as they'd learned during their first weeks of residence.

Marco helped gather the scattered fruit that had fallen from Eliza's basket during the boar encounter, his movements efficient but carefully maintaining physical distance between them. The walk back toward camp proceeded in charged silence, both acutely aware of the moment that had passed between them yet equally unwilling to acknowledge it directly.

They were perhaps halfway to camp when the storm announced itself with a sudden darkening of the sky and distant rumble of thunder. Marco assessed their position with quick efficiency.

"We won't make it back before the deluge," he concluded. "There's a rock outcropping ahead with adequate shelter. Better to wait it out than risk the path once it starts flowing."

The decision made, he led them on a slight detour from their usual route, arriving at a natural formation where erosion had carved a shallow cave into the hillside. They had barely entered this improvised shelter when the heavens opened, rain descending not in drops but in sheets that instantly transformed the jungle path into a small river.

"Good timing," Eliza observed, watching the downpour from their protected vantage point.

Marco nodded, setting down the fruit basket and creating deliberate space between them in the confined shelter. The cave was adequate for protection but hardly spacious, forcing a proximity that seemed suddenly fraught with significance after their earlier moment of connection.

The storm's intensity prevented normal conversation, thunder periodically crashing overhead with deafening force. They sat in companionable silence, watching nature's fury reshape the landscape beyond their shelter. There was something primal about the experience—two humans huddled against elemental power, stripped of technological buffers and social pretenses that typically mediated such encounters.

As the storm's initial violence gradually moderated to steady rainfall, the oppressive humidity that had preceded it dissipated, replaced by cooler air that carried the rich scents of wet vegetation and disturbed earth. Eliza found herself shivering slightly in her damp clothing, the temperature drop more noticeable after weeks of constant tropical heat.

"Here," Marco said, noticing her discomfort. He shifted closer, his body radiating warmth that invited rather than demanded proximity.

Eliza hesitated only briefly before accepting the offered heat, their shoulders touching as they sat side by side watching the continuing rainfall. The contact was innocent by any objective measure—necessary protection against cold—yet carried undercurrents neither could entirely ignore.

"I never thanked you properly," she said finally, breaking the extended silence. "Not just for today, but for everything since the shipwreck. We wouldn't have survived without you."

Marco's profile in the dim light showed the slight discomfort he typically displayed when faced with direct appreciation. "You've contributed more than you realize," he replied. "You adapted faster than most would in your circumstances."

The observation carried genuine respect rather than polite dismissal. Eliza found herself wondering how he had perceived her in those early days aboard the yacht—the pampered, decorative wife performing her assigned role with practiced precision.

"I was useless before," she admitted quietly. "Ornamental rather than functional. I didn't know I could be... more."

Marco turned slightly to study her face, his expression thoughtful rather than judgmental. "We rarely discover our capabilities until necessity demands their expression."

"Is that what happened with you?" Eliza asked, genuine curiosity overcoming the restraint that had characterized their previous conversations. "Leaving naval service for yacht crews?"

Something flickered in Marco's eyes—not anger at the personal question, but careful consideration of how much to reveal. The storm's continued presence created a strange intimacy between them, as if they existed temporarily outside normal time and social boundaries.

"My last deployment went bad," he said finally, gaze returning to the rainfall beyond their shelter. "Hostage extraction in a conflict zone. Intelligence failure led to an ambush. I lost three men under my command—good men with families, futures."

He paused, the memory clearly painful despite the neutral tone he maintained. "I received a commendation for getting the remaining team out alive, but it felt... hollow. Political considerations had overridden operational safety, and those men paid the price."

Eliza remained silent, recognizing the rare gift of genuine disclosure from this typically guarded man. Her hand found his in the dim light, a simple human connection offered without expectation.

"So you chose freedom," she said softly, echoing his earlier explanation of his career change.

Marco nodded, his fingers unconsciously intertwining with hers. "From responsibility for others' lives. From systems that value strategic objectives over individual welfare. The maritime industry offered escape—transient relationships, defined parameters, open horizons."

"And now?" Eliza asked, the question emerging before she could consider its implications. "Responsibility for our survival forced upon you by circumstance?"

His gaze returned to her face, something like rueful acknowledgment in his expression. "Different context. Immediate needs rather than abstract objectives. Keeping three people alive today, tomorrow—not executing policy decided by distant authorities."

The distinction revealed a philosophy Eliza had never encountered in her previous world of wealth and social positioning—a value system based on tangible impact rather than status or acquisition. In Marco's framework, meaning derived from immediate relationship to survival and welfare, not from accumulation or control.

"I've never lived that way," she admitted, the confession carrying vulnerability she would have hidden in her previous existence. "Everything was performance—the right appearance, connections, social position. Nothing felt... real."

"And now?" Marco echoed her earlier question, his voice softening as he studied her face in the dim light.

"Now everything is real," Eliza replied, the simple truth emerging without calculation. "Hunger, thirst, shelter, danger—there's no pretending, no performance that matters except actual capability."

"Does that frighten you?" he asked, genuine curiosity rather than challenge in the question.

Eliza considered before answering, her response thoughtful rather than automatic. "Less than it should. There's something... clarifying about necessity. The pretense falls away, leaving only what's genuine."

Their faces had drawn closer during this exchange, the intimacy of shared truth creating gravitational pull neither fully acknowledged. Rain continued falling beyond their shelter, creating a private world where normal boundaries seemed temporarily suspended.

"Like now," Marco observed quietly, his gaze dropping briefly to her lips before returning to her eyes with unmistakable question.

The moment balanced on knife's edge of possibility—Eliza acutely aware of multiple futures diverging from this single point of decision. The proper response, the loyal wife's reaction, would be retreat behind social convention and marital obligation. Yet in this rain-enclosed sanctuary, with danger just survived and adrenaline still coursing beneath her skin, those considerations seemed to belong to another woman in another life.

Without conscious decision, Eliza found herself leaning forward, closing the remaining distance between them. The first touch of their lips was hesitant, questioning—Marco's restraint evident even in this moment of surrender, giving her space to retreat if reality intruded on impulse.

What she hadn't anticipated was her own response—not the calculated passion she'd performed in her marriage, but something shockingly genuine that flared from casual touch to consuming need with breathtaking speed. Her hand rose instinctively to Marco's face, fingertips tracing the strong line of his jaw as the kiss deepened from tentative exploration to mutual hunger.

Marco's control remained evident even as desire clearly surged between them. His hand cradled her face with gentle reverence that contrasted with the unmistakable need in his response, his body leaning into hers without demanding or overwhelming. Unlike the entitled expectation she'd experienced from wealthy, powerful men, his desire asked rather than assumed, invited rather than claimed.

The distinction sent awareness spiraling through Eliza's body, awakening response more powerful than any she'd experienced in practiced seductions of her past. This wasn't performance but authentic connection—desire without agenda, passion without calculation.

When they finally separated, breath coming quick and uneven, the shock of genuine feeling left Eliza momentarily speechless. She had kissed men before—her husband thousands of times, others during her modeling years when circumstances required professional compliance—yet nothing had prepared her for this revelation of authentic desire.

"Eliza," Marco began, concern evident as he studied her stunned expression. "I shouldn't have—"

"No," she interrupted, finding her voice despite the confusion swirling through her mind. "Don't apologize. That was... I've never..."

Words failed as she struggled to articulate the paradigm shift occurring within her understanding of herself. How to explain that this seemingly simple physical connection had revealed the hollowness of every intimate encounter that preceded it? That for perhaps the first time in her adult life, desire had emerged from genuine feeling rather than strategic calculation?

Marco watched her with careful attention, neither pressing for resolution nor retreating from the intimacy they'd shared. Beyond their shelter, the storm was beginning to subside, reality gradually reasserting itself as rainfall lightened from deluge to gentle shower.

"We should head back soon," he said finally, giving her space to process what had passed between them. "Richard will be wondering where we are."

The mention of her husband landed like cold water on heated skin, returning Eliza abruptly to awareness of commitments and complications their momentary connection had temporarily suspended. Yes, she was married—bound by vows spoken before friends and clergy in a Manhattan cathedral, legal documents filed with appropriate authorities, social identity constructed around her status as Richard Harrington's wife.

Yet that marriage had existed in another reality—a world of wealth and social positioning where relationships served strategic purposes rather than emotional needs. Here on the island, stripped of artificial constructs and forced into authentic existence, different truths had emerged about herself, about Richard, about what constituted genuine connection between humans.

"Yes," she agreed finally, the single word acknowledging both practical necessity and unresolved complexity.

They gathered their belongings in silence, the fruit basket somehow intact despite the day's adventures. The rain had subsided enough for safe passage, though the jungle path would be slippery with mud and flowing water.

As they prepared to leave their temporary sanctuary, Marco paused, his expression serious in the dim light. "We should talk about what happened," he said quietly. "When you're ready."

The statement contained neither pressure nor dismissal—just acknowledgment that significant boundaries had been crossed, requiring eventual consideration regardless of immediate circumstances.

Eliza nodded, grateful for his understanding of her confusion yet unwilling to retreat entirely from the connection they'd established. "Yes," she agreed. "But not yet."

The walk back to camp proceeded in companionable silence, their bodies occasionally brushing against each other on the narrowed path without the previous careful distance Marco had maintained. Something fundamental had shifted between them—a door opened that could not be easily closed again, regardless of what rational consideration might eventually dictate.

Richard met them at the camp's edge, his expression shifting quickly from relief to suspicion as he observed their rain-soaked appearance and the subtle change in their dynamic.

"Where have you been?" he demanded, the question directed primarily at Eliza though his gaze darted between them. "I was about to search for you when the storm hit."

Marco stepped slightly away from Eliza, his posture resuming the professional distance that had characterized their earlier interactions. "Boar encounter in the eastern grove," he explained evenly. "Minor injury but nothing serious. We took shelter from the storm on the way back."

The factual account omitted significant emotional context while providing sufficient explanation for their delayed return. Eliza found herself both grateful for his discretion and disturbed by how easily they slipped into concealment—as if the authentic connection they'd shared minutes earlier could be compartmentalized away from daily reality.

Richard's gaze fixed on the bandage visible on Eliza's arm, his expression shifting from suspicion to concern. "Are you alright? Do we need antibiotics or something?"

The belated evidence of genuine care softened Eliza's conflicted emotions slightly. Despite his struggles with adaptation, despite the fundamental flaws in their marriage revealed by their changed circumstances, Richard was not a monster—just a man whose value systems had been rendered irrelevant by catastrophe.

"I'm fine," she assured him. "Marco treated it properly. Just a scratch."

Her husband nodded, attention already shifting from immediate concern to logistical considerations. "I've moved everything under shelter. The rain leaked through in the back section, but I managed to keep most things dry."

The simple statement represented perhaps the most significant contribution Richard had made to their survival since the shipwreck—actual productive assistance rather than nominal supervision or complaint. Eliza felt a surge of conflicted emotion at this evidence that adaptation, however reluctant, might still be possible for him.

"Thank you," she acknowledged, the gratitude genuine despite the emotional maelstrom still swirling beneath her calm exterior.

As they moved toward the shelter to dry themselves and prepare the evening meal, Eliza became acutely conscious of standing at a crossroads whose significance transcended mere physical survival. The kiss in the cave had revealed possibilities her previous existence had never allowed her to consider—authentic connection based on genuine respect and mutual capability rather than transaction and performance.

Yet commitments remained, obligations established in another life but still binding in this one. Richard was her husband, whatever the flaws in their relationship might be. Social convention, legal obligation, moral consideration—all argued for restraint and reconsideration regardless of newly awakened desire.

Marco maintained careful distance as they moved through their evening routines, his respect for her conflicted position evident in every interaction. No pressure, no expectation, no attempt to influence her processing of what had passed between them—just quiet presence and a continued practical support as they prepared to end another day on the island.

As darkness fell and they retreated to their separate sleeping spaces within the shared shelter, Eliza found herself acutely aware of the men's proximity—Richard's familiar presence representing security and obligation, Marco's newer but increasingly essential connection promising authenticity she had never experienced in her previous life.

No simple resolution presented itself as sleep gradually claimed her exhausted body. The only certainty emerging from a day of danger, revelation, and awakening was that whatever path she ultimately chose would reshape her understanding of herself in ways that could never be undone.

The island had stripped away artificial constructs of her previous existence, revealing truths about her capabilities, her desires, and her fundamental nature that civilization had allowed her to ignore. Whether those revelations represented liberation or complication remained to be determined—a question whose answer would emerge not from social expectation but from the authentic self gradually awakening beneath years of careful performance.

CHAPTER NINE

Shifting Alliances

Eliza stared at the shelter's thatched ceiling, her mind replaying the cave moment in endless loops. The rational part of her brain attempted to categorize it—a survival response, an adrenaline-fueled mistake, a moment of weakness in extreme circumstances.

"It meant nothing," she whispered to herself in the darkness. "Pure biology. Fear and relief mixed together."

But her heartbeat quickened at the memory of Marco's touch, betraying her attempts at clinical analysis. She rolled to her side, pulling the makeshift blanket tighter despite the tropical heat.

From his corner of the shelter, Richard's familiar snoring provided a counterpoint to her churning thoughts. She'd known that sound for many years—a soundtrack to comfortable predictability, to clearly defined roles and expectations. Now it felt like an echo from another life.

Her fingers traced the bandage on her arm where Marco had treated her wound. She tried to frame the kiss as tactical—a way to secure his continued protection and expertise. The thought made her stomach turn. She wasn't that person, had never been that calculating.

The truth rose unbidden, impossible to suppress. Marco's presence awakened something she'd buried so deep she'd forgotten its existence. Not just attraction—though that burned fierce enough—but a recognition of possibility. Of who she could be when stripped of society's careful labels and boxes.

In their previous life, she'd been Richard's wife, the perfect corporate spouse, her identity carefully curated to complement his. But here, working alongside Marco, she'd discovered strength she never knew she possessed. Capability. Agency.

The kiss hadn't created these feelings—it had simply crystallized what had been building since the moment he'd guided them through the deadly surf to shore. In Marco's eyes, she saw herself reflected not as an accessory or a role, but as a whole person. The realization terrified and thrilled her in equal measure.

She pressed her palms against her eyes, as if the physical pressure could suppress the unwanted epiphany. But the truth remained, undeniable in the quiet darkness: Marco made her feel alive in ways she never knew were possible.

The morning brought renewed purpose as Marco outlined plans to reinforce their shelter against incoming weather. Eliza found herself volunteering before Richard could voice his usual complaints.

"We'll need more palm fronds." Marco demonstrated the weaving technique. "Like this—see how they lock together?"

Their hands brushed as she took the frond. Her pulse jumped, but she forced herself to maintain professional distance. "Show me again?"

Hours passed in comfortable silence broken by occasional questions and observations. They developed an unspoken rhythm—Marco cutting, Eliza weaving, their movements synchronized without effort.

Richard paced the beach's edge. "This is pointless. We should focus on rescue signals."

"The shelter keeps us alive until rescue comes." Eliza's voice carried a new edge of confidence. "Want to help?"

"I'll leave the manual labor to those better suited." He wandered off toward their water collection point.

Marco didn't comment on the exchange, but his slight head shake spoke volumes. He reached past her to adjust a loose section, his presence solid and warm at her back. "You're getting good at this."

"Had a good teacher." She meant it to sound casual but heard the underlying warmth in her voice.

"Look." He pointed to her completed section. "Perfect tension. You've got natural instincts."

The praise felt different from Richard's calculated compliments at corporate functions. This was earned, genuine. She found herself smiling, really smiling, for what felt like the first time in years.

A palm frond slipped, tickling her neck. She laughed—a real laugh, not the polite society chuckle she'd perfected. Marco joined in, the sound rich and unrestrained.

The moment stretched between them, charged with possibility. But Marco stepped back, giving her space she hadn't known she needed. His respect for her situation, his refusal to press the advantage, only intensified the pull she felt toward him.

The afternoon sun beat down as they continued reinforcing the shelter. Eliza reached for another palm frond, her hand landing on Marco's. The contact sent electricity through her arm, but she didn't pull away. His skin felt rough, weathered, real against hers.

Marco's breath caught. Their eyes met, and the pretense of casual cooperation shattered. He drew her closer, or maybe she moved toward him—the distinction blurred as their bodies came together.

Her arms wrapped around his neck without conscious thought. His embrace lifted her off her feet, strong and sure, nothing like Richard's careful, measured affection. A sound escaped her throat, raw and unplanned.

"I shouldn't—" But her body betrayed her words, pressing closer.

The world narrowed to sensations: Marco's heartbeat against her chest, the salt-tang of his skin, the way his hands splayed across her back. She felt untethered, floating free of the careful restraints she'd built around herself.

This wasn't the calculated passion of her marriage, where every touch served a purpose, every kiss carried expectations. This was pure, primal connection—desire without framework or rules.

She recognized herself in this moment with startling clarity. Not Eliza the corporate wife, not the carefully curated image she'd maintained for years. Just Eliza, wanting and wanted, real and raw and alive.

Her fingers traced the curve of his shoulder, marveling at her own boldness. No performance, no mental checklist of appropriate responses. Just pure instinct, pure feeling.

Marco's hand cupped her face, thumb tracing her cheekbone. The tenderness of it nearly undid her. She'd forgotten touch could feel like this—honest, unguarded, free of agenda.

"Eliza." Her name on his lips sounded different, like he saw through every layer to her core.

She trembled, not from fear but from the intensity of being truly seen, truly known for the first time in years. The island had stripped away her careful facades, revealing a woman she barely recognized but instantly trusted.

A twig snapped in the distance. Marco and Eliza broke apart, their breathing ragged. Footsteps crunched through leaves, growing closer.

"Found more coconuts." Richard's voice carried through the trees. "Though I don't see why we need—"

Eliza stepped back, smoothing her hair. Her hands shook as she picked up a fallen palm frond. Marco moved to the opposite side of the shelter, his jaw tight.

Richard emerged from the treeline, coconuts tucked under his arms. He dropped them near the water collection point with a dull thud. "Making progress with our little hut?"

"Almost done with the north side." Eliza's voice sounded strange in her ears, too high, too brittle.

While Richard launched into another complaint about their primitive conditions, Eliza's mind raced. The kiss burned in her memory, impossible to dismiss as mere survival instinct this time. She'd chosen it, wanted it, initiated it with full awareness.

She watched Richard gesture about proper rescue protocols, his familiar mannerisms suddenly foreign. Their years of marriage crystallized into sharp focus – the careful scripts, the measured responses, the roles they'd assigned each other. She'd spent so long molding herself to fit his expectations that she'd forgotten who she was beneath the performance.

But here, stripped of social constraints, she'd discovered truth in Marco's arms. Not just passion, but recognition. He saw her strength, her capability, her raw essence. With him, she didn't have to pretend or perform or carefully curate her responses.

The realization settled in her chest, heavy with implications. This wasn't about marriage vows or social obligations. This was about authenticity – about finally acknowledging the woman she'd buried under years of compromise.

Her fingers traced the rough edge of the palm frond, its texture grounding her in the present moment. She'd spent so long doing what was expected. Maybe survival meant more than just staying alive. Maybe it meant choosing to truly live.

Richard watched Eliza and Marco working together by the fire pit, their movements synchronized like dancers who'd rehearsed for years. His jaw clenched at their easy laughter, so different from the polite chuckles Eliza reserved for his business dinners.

"We need to talk." He caught her arm as she passed with an armload of firewood. "Privately."

Eliza followed him down the beach, out of Marco's earshot. The setting sun painted her face in shades of gold, highlighting changes he hadn't noticed before—a new confidence in her posture, a wildness in her eyes.

"You're getting awfully cozy with the deck hand."

"He's teaching me essential skills, Richard. We need to survive."

"Is that what you call it?" He stepped closer. "I've seen how you look at him."

"Don't be ridiculous." But her eyes slid away from his. "He knows this environment. We'd be dead without him."

"And what happens when we're rescued? When we return to our life?" Richard straightened his spine, summoning the boardroom authority that had served him so well. "Remember who you are, Eliza. The house in the Hamptons, the summer galas, your charity board position—that's your world. Not this primitive crap."

"I haven't forgotten anything." Her voice carried a new steel he'd never heard before.

"Good. Because once we're back, I'm thinking CEO within five years. The Anderson merger is practically guaranteed." He touched her cheek, the gesture possessive. "We've built something remarkable together. Don't throw it away over some... survival fantasy."

Eliza stepped back from his touch. "I'm not throwing anything away. I'm just trying to stay alive."

"By clinging to him?"

"By learning to be useful. To contribute." She gestured at the shelter. "Like I've been doing since we landed here."

Richard's laugh held no humor. "Contributing? Playing jungle girl with a glorified cabin boy?"

"He has a name. And skills we need."

"For now." Richard's smile turned cold. "But remember who holds the real power once we're back in civilization."

CHAPTER TEN

Claiming Territory

T he morning sun filtered through the jungle canopy as Eliza shouldered the makeshift basket she'd woven from palm fronds. Marco checked the sharpened stick he'd fashioned into a spear.

"We'll try the northern part of the island today." Marco traced a path in the dirt. "I spotted some fruit trees there yesterday."

"I'll join you." Richard stepped out of the shelter.

"Someone needs to tend the signal fire." Marco's voice held no room for debate. "The smoke has to stay visible."

Richard's face darkened. "My wife isn't going alone with—"

"I'll be fine." Eliza cut him off. "We need food, Richard. Real food, not just coconuts."

They headed into the jungle, leaving Richard by the smoking fire. The forest embraced them in its green shadows, alive with bird calls and rustling leaves. Marco moved with silent grace, teaching Eliza to spot edible plants and animal tracks.

Behind them, branches cracked softly as Richard stealthily crept in their wake.

"Here." Marco pointed to some scratches on a tree trunk. "Wild pigs passed through recently."

They followed the trail until it opened into a hidden clearing. They stumbled upon the clearing while foraging for fruit, the sound of rushing water drawing them deeper into the jungle until they pushed through a curtain of vines and found themselves in paradise. A small waterfall tumbled down moss-covered rocks into a crystal-clear pool, sunlight dappling through the canopy above to create shifting patterns across the lush ground.

"Oh my God," Eliza breathed, taking in the beauty of the hidden sanctuary. "This is incredible."

Marco stood beside her, his eyes sweeping across the clearing before settling on her face. "It's perfect," he said, his voice low and warm.

Eliza walked toward the pool, feeling the soft moss beneath her feet. It was like a natural carpet, springy and thick. "It feels like we're the first people to ever find this place."

"Maybe we are," Marco said, following her to the water's edge. He knelt down, dipping his hand into the pool. "It's warm."

Eliza turned to look at him, suddenly aware of their solitude in a way that sent a flutter through her stomach. For weeks, they'd been dancing around what was growing between them, careful to maintain appropriate boundaries despite the obvious attraction. Here, away from Richard's watchful eyes and the constraints of their makeshift camp, those boundaries felt paper-thin.

"I've been thinking about you," she said suddenly, the words tumbling out before she could stop them. "About us."

Marco stood, water dripping from his fingertips as he faced her. The look in his eyes made her heart race. "I think about you too," he admitted. "More than I should."

"What's stopping us?" Eliza asked, gesturing around at the pristine clearing. "Out here, all those rules feel so... meaningless."

Marco stepped closer, close enough that she could feel the heat radiating from his body. "Are you sure, Eliza? I need to know you're certain."

Instead of answering with words, she reached up and placed her palm against his cheek. The stubble beneath her fingers felt nothing like Richard's once smooth, pampered skin. Marco was real, substantial, his strength coming from actual capability rather than social position.

"I've never been more sure of anything," she whispered.

When their lips met, it wasn't hesitant or questioning like their previous stolen moments. This kiss held certainty, a decision made and embraced. Marco's arms encircled her waist, pulling her against him with a strength that made her feel simultaneously safe and dizzyingly aware of him as a man.

"I've wanted to do that for so long," he murmured against her mouth.

Eliza smiled, her hands sliding up to his shoulders. "Just that?"

Marco's laugh was low and rich. "No," he admitted. "Not just that."

His hands moved up her sides, touch gentle yet confident in a way Richard's had never been. When his thumbs brushed the sides of her breasts, even through her worn shirt, Eliza felt a jolt of electricity run straight through her body.

"Can I touch you?" he asked, his voice husky. "Really touch you?"

The question itself was a revelation. Richard had never asked—he'd simply taken what he considered his right. Marco's request acknowledged her as a person with choices, not a possession to be used.

"Yes," she breathed. "Please."

From the shadow of a breadfruit tree, Richard watched, his hands balled into fists.

With surprising tenderness for hands so strong, Marco began to lift her shirt. Each newly exposed inch of skin received attention—a brush of his fingertips, a soft kiss, a gentle breath that raised goosebumps despite the tropical heat.

"You're beautiful," he said, and unlike Richard's calculated compliments designed to ensure compliance, Marco's words held genuine wonder. When her shirt finally fell away, his intake of breath was audible. "So beautiful."

Eliza reached for him, tugging at his own shirt with new-found boldness. "I want to see you too."

Together they shed the barriers between them, clothing discarded on the moss until they stood naked in the dappled sunlight. Marco's body was a revelation—strong from actual work rather than performative gym sessions, scarred in places from real experiences rather than cosmetically perfected.

"You're staring," he said with a half-smile.

"So are you," she countered, feeling oddly comfortable in her nakedness despite the openness of the clearing. With Richard, she'd always felt evaluated, judged. With Marco, she felt appreciated.

He held out his hand. "Come here."

Marco led her to a patch of moss near the water, thick and soft beneath their bodies as they sank down together. His hand cupped her face as he kissed her again, deeper now, his tongue meeting hers in a dance that sent heat pooling low in her belly.

"I don't want to rush this," he murmured against her throat as his lips traced a path downward. "Tell me what feels good."

Eliza almost laughed at the question—not from humor but from surprise. No one had ever asked her that before. Sex with Richard had been a performance, a transaction. This... this was a conversation between bodies.

"Everything you're doing feels good," she said honestly. "Just don't stop touching me."

Marco's hand skimmed down her side, over the curve of her hip. "Like this?"

"Yes," she breathed.

His mouth found her breast, and Eliza gasped at the sensation. Unlike Richard's mechanical attentions—always the same pattern, always rushed through as a mere checkpoint on the way to his own pleasure—Marco approached her body with genuine curiosity. When she responded strongly to something, he noticed and built upon it.

"You like that," he observed, not a question but a discovery.

"God, yes," she managed, her fingers threading through his hair.

His exploration continued downward, lips and tongue tracing paths across her stomach, her hips, the sensitive skin of her inner thighs. Each touch built upon the last, creating a symphony of sensation unlike anything she'd experienced before.

When his mouth finally found the center of her desire, Eliza cried out, the sound echoing off the rocks around the waterfall. Marco looked up, his eyes meeting hers in silent question.

"Don't you dare stop," she said, her voice shaking.

His smile was quick before he returned to his task, his tongue finding rhythms that seemed perfectly attuned to her body's responses. Unlike Richard's one-size-fits-all approach to intimacy, Marco paid attention, adjusting based on her reactions, building pleasure in waves that grew increasingly intense.

"Marco," she gasped, feeling something building inside her that transcended any physical pleasure she'd known before. "Oh God, Marco—"

The climax crashed over her like the waterfall itself, powerful and overwhelming, washing away everything except the feeling of his mouth against her most sensitive flesh and the waves of pleasure radiating outward through her entire body.

As she gradually returned to awareness, she found Marco watching her with an expression that held equal parts desire and tenderness.

"That was the most beautiful thing I've ever seen," he said, moving up to lie beside her.

"I've never felt anything like that before," she admitted, turning to face him. "Not even close."

A shadow of understanding crossed his face. "Never?"

Eliza shook her head. "Sex has always been... mechanical. A thing to get through, not something to experience."

Marco brushed a strand of hair from her face. "That's not what it should be."

"I'm learning that," she said, her hand trailing down his chest, feeling the rapid beat of his heart beneath her palm. "Show me more?"

His smile was both tender and hungry. "Are you sure? We don't have to go further."

In answer, Eliza guided his hand back to her body. "I want everything with you."

Marco kissed her deeply as his fingers resumed their exploration, finding her still sensitive from her first release. "Tell me if anything doesn't feel good," he murmured.

But everything did feel good—impossibly, extraordinarily good. His touch was both confident and considerate, building her desire again rather than rushing toward his own satisfaction. When he finally positioned himself above her, the question was clear in his eyes.

"Yes," she whispered, reaching up to pull him closer.

When their bodies joined, Eliza felt a completeness she'd never experienced before. Sex with Richard had always been a disconnected act, bodies going through motions while minds remained separate. This was union—not just physical but something deeper.

"You feel amazing," Marco said, his voice rough with emotion. "Eliza..."

They began to move together, finding a rhythm as natural as the waterfall's flow. Marco's strength was evident in every controlled movement, yet he never used it to dominate or overwhelm. Instead, it served them both, supporting his weight, allowing him to adjust angle and depth in response to her reactions.

"Is this good?" he asked, his breathing ragged.

"Better than good," she managed, her hands clutching his shoulders. "Don't stop."

Unlike Richard's predictable pattern—always the same positions, always focused on his own pleasure—Marco seemed genuinely invested in discovering what brought her joy. When he shifted slightly and her breath caught, he repeated the movement, building on what worked rather than following a script.

To her amazement, Eliza felt that building tension returning, stronger than before. "Marco," she gasped, "I think I'm going to—"

"Yes," he encouraged, his hand sliding between them to increase her pleasure. "Let go, Eliza. I've got you."

The second climax was even more powerful than the first, a release that seemed to shatter her into a thousand pieces before putting her back together as someone new. Marco followed moments later, his face revealing a vulnerability she'd never seen in him before, a moment of complete openness as pleasure overtook him.

They remained joined afterward, foreheads touching, breath mingling as they gradually returned to themselves. The waterfall's gentle music filled the silence, a natural soundtrack to the most profound experience of Eliza's life.

"I never knew," she said eventually, her voice soft with wonder. "That it could be like that. So... connected."

Marco brushed his lips against hers tenderly. "That's what it's supposed to be. Not a performance or a transaction. Just two people truly seeing each other."

As they lay together afterward on the soft moss, bodies cooling in the gentle breeze that stirred the clearing, Eliza felt a profound shift in her understanding of intimacy. What she'd experienced with Richard all those years had been a hollow imitation of what was possible between two people who genuinely cared for each other.

"We should probably head back soon," Marco said eventually, though he made no move to disentangle himself from her.

Eliza nodded, reality gradually reasserting itself. "Richard will be wondering where we are."

"Do you regret this?" Marco asked, his eyes searching hers.

She thought about it honestly, considering the complications that would inevitably follow, the difficult conversations ahead, the uncertain future they faced both on the island and beyond. Yet the answer came with surprising clarity.

"No," she said firmly. "I don't regret a single moment."

Richard stumbled back through the jungle, his feet catching on roots and vines. His hands trembled as he pushed through the undergrowth, no longer caring about the scratches from thorns or the mud staining his clothes.

Back at the shelter, he paced the small clearing like a caged animal. The signal fire crackled, forgotten and untended. His mind raced with images of what he'd witnessed - Eliza, his wife, with that... that savage.

He kicked over the stack of collected firewood, scattering it across the sand. The physical outlet did nothing to quell the rage building inside him. All his life, Richard had owned things - companies, properties, people. Eliza was his, purchased with a lifestyle she could never have achieved on her own. How dare she give herself to someone else?

"I'll destroy him," he muttered, running his hands through his disheveled hair. "I'll destroy them both."

As Marco reluctantly dressed and prepared to return to camp, Eliza knew something fundamental had changed—not just in her relationship with Marco, but in her understanding of herself. The woman who had boarded the Aurora weeks ago, concerned with appearances and status and playing her assigned role, seemed like a stranger now.

Whatever happened next—whether rescue came tomorrow or months from now—she could never go back to being that woman again. And looking at Marco, at the man who had shown her what real connection felt like, she found she didn't want to.

Richard's face contorted as Eliza and Marco emerged from the jungle path. He stormed across the beach, pointing an accusatory finger. "You whore! I saw everything at the waterfall."

Eliza froze, her stomach dropping. The peaceful afterglow shattered like glass.

"All this time, playing the dutiful wife while spreading your legs for him?" Richard's voice cracked with rage. "I'll have you both ruined when we're rescued. You'll never work again," he jabbed a finger at Marco. "And you," he turned to Eliza, "can forget about the prenup settlement."

Marco stepped forward, his posture relaxed but alert. "Those threats might work in your world, Richard. But out here? Your money means nothing. Your influence means nothing."

"You dare speak to me? You're just the help!" Richard lunged forward.

Marco didn't flinch. "I'm the reason we're alive. The reason you eat. The reason you have shelter."

Eliza's hands trembled, but her voice stayed steady. "He's right, Richard. Everything between us was a transaction. I traded my freedom for security, my identity for status." She took a deep breath. "I won't apologize for finding something real."

"Real?" Richard laughed, the sound brittle. "You think this island fantasy will last? That he can give you the life you're accustomed to?"

"The life I was trapped in," Eliza corrected. "I don't want that life anymore. I don't want to be that person."

Richard's facade of sophisticated businessman crumbled completely. He kicked at the sand like a child, spittle flying from his lips. "You're mine! I own you!"

"You never owned me," Eliza said. "You just made me forget who I was."

Marco remained steady beside her, not touching but present. His silence spoke volumes - no grand declarations, no posturing, just quiet strength.

The truth hung between them, stripped bare like the island itself. Three people with nowhere to hide, no social masks to wear, no pretenses left to maintain. Just raw humanity, for better or worse.

The next morning, Marco shouldered his makeshift pack. "I'm moving to the western cove. Better fishing there, more shelter from storms."

Eliza watched him gather his few possessions - the knife he'd salvaged, lengths of rope, palm fronds he'd woven into tools. Her decision crystallized with each item he collected.

"I'm coming with you." She began gathering her own things.

Richard scrambled up from his spot in the shade. "Like hell you are. This is ridiculous - we need to stay together."

"No, Richard. We need to survive. And I've learned more about that from Marco in weeks than from you in years." Eliza's voice held no anger, just certainty.

Marco nodded toward the eastern side of the island. "There's good water near the rocks there, Richard. Plenty of fruit trees. You'll manage."

"You can't just-" Richard sputtered, but Marco was already heading down the beach, Eliza falling into step beside him.

They established their new camp where the western cove curved inward, protected by natural rock formations. Within hours, Marco had constructed a more stable shelter than their original shared one, while Eliza set up a smoking rack for fish.

The island's natural features seemed to reinforce their separation. A ridge of volcanic rock cut across the middle, creating distinct territories. The western side offered rich fishing grounds and natural protection, while the eastern section held more fruit trees but remained exposed to the elements.

Richard's complaints echoed across the divide for the first few days, but necessity forced him to adapt. They occasionally glimpsed him foraging or attempting to fish, his designer clothes now permanently stained and torn.

The physical distance reflected their new reality. Marco and Eliza's side of the island hummed with purpose - improved shelters, food preservation, even a garden of salvaged plants. Richard's territory remained sparse, marked only by his basic needs for survival.

Sunlight filtered through the palm leaf roof of their new shelter, painting warm patterns across the sleeping area. Eliza blinked awake slowly, feeling Marco's arm draped over her waist, his chest warm against her back. For the first time since the shipwreck, she didn't wake up tense. There was something amazing about not having Richard's eyes on them, judging every interaction.

She shifted carefully, turning to face Marco without waking him. He looked different when he slept – younger somehow, the constant alertness gone from his features. That perpetual watchfulness that kept them all alive day after day had slipped away in sleep, revealing a vulnerability she rarely got to see.

The thin blanket had slipped down during the night, exposing his chest and stomach. Marco's body had changed over their weeks on the island, growing leaner and more defined from the constant physical work. So different from Richard's carefully maintained gym physique – this was strength with purpose, earned through actual survival.

As her eyes wandered lower, she noticed his body's natural morning response beneath the remaining blanket. The sight triggered something in her that felt new and unfamiliar – not the calculated "oh, I should do something about that" she'd felt with Richard, but an actual desire that caught her by surprise.

Eliza hesitated. With Richard, moments like this had always been transactions. She'd perform for him, he'd be in a better mood later, maybe more generous with his credit card or his attention. Every intimate moment had a price tag, an expected return on investment.

But Marco was still asleep. He wasn't asking for anything. Whatever she chose to do now would be just because she wanted to. The realization was both freeing and a little scary – without the script she'd followed for years, she'd have to trust her own desires, many of which she'd buried so deep she barely recognized them anymore.

Moving carefully, she slipped down beneath the blanket. She pressed her lips against his chest, feeling his heartbeat quicken under her touch. When she finally took him into her mouth, it wasn't the efficient, practiced motion she'd perfected with Richard – just the simple pleasure of making someone happy, someone who had shown her nothing but kindness and respect.

Marco woke gradually. She felt the moment awareness hit him – his breath catching, his hand finding her hair. He didn't grip or guide, just gently ran his fingers through the strands, a touch that felt more like connection than control.

"Eliza," he murmured, her name sounding like a question and an appreciation all at once.

She looked up, meeting his eyes with a smile. "Good morning."

The tenderness in his face made her heart skip. Without a word, he gently guided her back up until they were face to face.

"That's quite a way to wake up," he said, voice still husky with sleep. His fingers traced her cheek softly. "But I'd rather share this with you."

The comment struck her hard. Even now, with her initiating, Marco was thinking about shared pleasure rather than just taking what was offered. With Richard, it had always been about what she could do for him, not what they could experience together.

"I wanted to," she said simply, surprised by how true it was. No calculation, no performance – just genuine desire.

Marco smiled – that rare, full smile that transformed his usually serious face – and pulled her into a kiss that quickly deepened. His hands moved over her body with appreciation rather than entitlement, each touch drawing reactions she couldn't have faked if she tried.

As their bodies came together, Eliza found herself responding in ways that shocked her. No mental checklist of appropriate sounds or expressions, no careful monitoring of her reactions – just feeling everything as it happened.

"You're so beautiful," Marco whispered against her neck.

Unlike Richard's evaluating comments about her body – always with an undercurrent of "maintain this or else" – Marco's words felt like pure appreciation, with no strings attached. The difference sent a fresh wave of desire through her that was entirely real, not manufactured.

When his hand slipped between them to touch her more intimately, Eliza gasped at the intensity.

"I don't—" she started, confused by feelings stronger than anything she'd experienced before. "I've never felt like this—"

"Don't think about it," Marco encouraged, his eyes holding hers. "Just feel it. You don't have to perform for me."

It was like he'd read her mind, naming exactly what had held her back all these years. As they moved together, finding a perfect rhythm without any direction or management, she let go of the mental control she'd always maintained during sex.

Her climax caught her by surprise, genuine rather than faked, so intense that for a moment she couldn't think at all. Marco followed shortly after, his expression open and vulnerable in a way she'd never seen before.

Afterward, she found herself trembling slightly against him, aftershocks still running through her body. Marco held her close, his arms protective but not possessive.

"That was..." she tried, failing to find words for what had just happened.

"I know," he said simply.

They lay together quietly as the morning light grew stronger. Unlike with Richard – where sex ended with immediate separation, him checking his phone or heading to the shower – Marco seemed content to just be with her, neither of them rushing to break the connection.

"I didn't know it could be like that," Eliza finally admitted. "So real."

Marco looked at her thoughtfully. "Most people put on some kind of act during sex," he said. "It feels safer than being truly vulnerable."

His observation hit home, making her realize this pattern went beyond just Richard. Her whole understanding of intimacy had been built around performance rather than genuine connection.

"How did you learn to be different?" she asked.

Marco thought for a moment before answering. "Being in life-or-death situations changes you," he said. "In the military, you learn pretty quickly that pretending doesn't matter when things get critical. What matters is real connection with the people you're depending on."

It made sense – their situation on the island had done something similar, stripping away the social masks they normally wore and forcing them to be real with each other.

"I still catch myself calculating sometimes," she confessed. "Like I'm about to say what I think you want to hear instead of what I actually feel."

"Old habits don't disappear overnight," Marco said, no judgment in his voice. "It takes time to feel safe enough to be real with someone. To trust that they won't use your real reactions against you later."

As they finally got up to start their day, Eliza felt different in a way that went beyond just physical satisfaction. She'd gotten a glimpse of something she never knew was possible – a connection not based on what she could get or what was expected of her, but on genuine feeling.

Whatever happened next – whether rescue came tomorrow or months from now – she knew she could never go back to being the woman who boarded the Aurora. That carefully crafted socialite was gone, as thoroughly sunk as the yacht itself. In her place was someone newer, more real, and much more alive.

A month passed, marked by the crude calendar Eliza had scratched into a piece of driftwood, each line representing another day of their transformed existence. The island had reshaped them all, their bodies adapting to this raw existence in different ways, molding them like clay into more elemental versions of themselves.

Eliza studied her reflection in a still pool near their shelter, the water crystal clear in the morning light. Her skin had deepened to a rich bronze, far from the careful tanning sessions she'd once scheduled with her exclusive aesthetician. The designer highlights in her hair had grown out, replaced by natural sun-bleaching that created subtle variations of gold. Without access to her extensive beauty routine, her face had simplified - clear skin from clean living and physical work, genuine smile lines around her eyes that spoke of real joy rather than practiced charm.

"You look different," Marco said, coming up behind her, his feet silent on the packed earth. His own transformation was striking - his already athletic frame had grown more defined, muscles hardened from constant physical labor. Scars and calluses marked his hands, telling the story of their survival through daily struggles with wood, stone, and sea.

"Good different?" She touched her face, still adjusting to this new version of herself, fingers tracing unfamiliar contours.

"Real different." He traced a finger along her shoulder, following a pattern of freckles that had emerged in the sun, spreading like constellations across her skin. "No more artificial layers."

Across the island, they spotted Richard during one of their foraging trips, a distant figure moving between the trees. He'd lost the soft edges of privilege, his expensive clothes hanging loose on his frame like forgotten banners of his former life. The weight loss had aged him, deepening the lines of bitterness around his mouth, making him appear more haunted than distinguished.

"Look at us," Eliza mused later that evening, as she and Marco prepared their dinner of fresh fish and foraged greens. "Nature doesn't care about Botox or personal trainers or designer diets. It just... reshapes you according to its own rules, stripping away everything superficial."

"Into what we're meant to be," Marco added, his hand finding the small of her back, warm and steady. "Not what society sculpted us into."

The thought struck her - how much energy she'd spent maintaining an artificial version of herself, chasing an impossible ideal through expensive treatments and careful manipulation, when this stronger, simpler beauty had been waiting underneath all along, requiring only honesty to emerge.

CHAPTER ELEVEN

Storms Within

Eliza sat alone by the shoreline, waves lapping at her feet as the sun dipped toward the horizon. Her fingers traced patterns in the sand, unconsciously drawing the infinity loops she used to doodle during endless charity luncheons, back when every pen stroke had been a calculated act of appearing appropriately distracted but still engaged.

Those memories felt like scenes from someone else's life now. She remembered the calculated smiles, the strategic seating arrangements, the careful management of Richard's business connections through perfectly orchestrated dinner parties. Each gesture had been a move in an elaborate game of social chess, each conversation a delicate balance of flattery and subtle information gathering that had left her mentally exhausted but outwardly poised.

"You're perfect at this," Richard had told her once, after she'd smoothed over a potential business crisis with just the right combination of charm and subtle manipulation. Not 'you're perfect' - but perfect at maintaining their carefully constructed world. She could still see his approving smile, the way his eyes had gleamed with satisfaction at having such a useful asset in his wife.

A tear rolled down her cheek, surprising her. When was the last time she'd cried without calculating the effect it would have on others? Here on the beach, nobody was watching. Nobody to impress. Nobody to manipulate. The salt spray mixed with her tears until she couldn't tell which was which.

Her heart raced when she thought of Marco - not the controlled flutter she'd trained herself to display at appropriate moments, but a wild, untamed thing that frightened her with its intensity. She hadn't planned this, couldn't control it, couldn't turn it into another social advantage. The raw honesty of her feelings for him defied every rule she'd ever learned about keeping her emotions in check.

"Get it together," she whispered to herself, her old self-preservation instincts kicking in. Feelings made you vulnerable. Vulnerability got you hurt. She'd learned that lesson early and built her life around avoiding it, constructing elaborate defenses that had served her well in the cutthroat world of high society.

But the walls she'd constructed so carefully were crumbling in the face of Marco's quiet strength and unflinching honesty. He saw through her practiced smiles, waited patiently through her reflexive deflections, until the real Eliza had no choice but to emerge. His gentle persistence was like waves wearing away at a cliff face, inevitable and unstoppable.

The thought terrified her. She'd spent so long being whatever others needed her to be, she wasn't sure she knew who she really was anymore. What if Marco saw the real her and walked away? What if the authentic Eliza wasn't enough? The questions swirled in her mind like the tide pools at her feet, deep and dangerous.

She pressed her hands against her chest, feeling her heart beat its unfamiliar rhythm of genuine emotion. This wasn't the carefully choreographed dance of her old life. This was free fall, exhilarating and terrifying in equal measure. The setting sun painted the waves in shades of gold and pink, as if nature itself was celebrating her tentative steps toward authenticity.

Marco stripped bark from fallen branches, his hands working with practiced efficiency while his mind wandered. The physical labor grounded him, kept him focused when his thoughts threatened to spiral into dangerous territory. But even as he crafted rope from plant fibers, Eliza's smile kept appearing in his mind - not her polished society smile, but the real one that emerged when she mastered a new survival skill.

His chest tightened at the memory of her triumph when she'd successfully started her first fire. No diamonds or designer clothes could match the pure joy that had radiated from her face in that moment. She'd stripped away the artificial layers of her wealthy existence, revealing the extraordinary woman beneath. The way her hands had trembled with excitement, smudged with ash and honest effort, told him more about her true character than any society column ever could.

The rope took shape between his fingers as he imagined teaching her more, building a life together that centered on genuine connection rather than material possessions. He'd show her how to read weather patterns, navigate by stars, find beauty in simple moments that couldn't be bought. Each lesson would be another thread binding them together, weaving a future from trust and shared discovery.

"Money can't create what we have," he murmured to himself, testing the strength of his newly made rope. Their bond had formed through shared challenges and mutual respect, not social climbing or financial transactions. He'd earned her trust through competence and character, not credit cards and connections. The calluses on his hands were worth more than any golden handshake.

Richard's presence nagged at the edges of his consciousness, but Marco dismissed the wealthy man's claims on Eliza. He'd seen the way she looked at her husband now - with the clear-eyed assessment of someone awakening from a long sleep. The polished veneer of their marriage had cracked, revealing its hollow core. Every false smile and rehearsed gesture between them only highlighted the authenticity of what he shared with Eliza.

His hands stilled on the rope as he remembered Eliza's face when she'd watched him navigate the raft through the storm. There had been no pretense in her expression, no calculated

assessment of social advantage. Just raw admiration and growing trust that transcended their different backgrounds. The rain
had washed away all pretense, leaving only truth between them.

Pride swelled in his chest. He'd crossed the invisible barriers
of class not through wealth or status, but by being exactly who
he was. Each genuine moment between them was worth more
than all the luxury she'd left behind. In teaching her survival
skills, he'd shown her how to truly live, and that revelation was
priceless.

Richard crouched behind a cluster of palms, watching Marco
and Eliza gather firewood. His once manicured nails dug into
his palms as Eliza laughed at something Marco said. That laugh
- once reserved for his witty remarks at cocktail parties - now
belonged to someone else. The sound of it twisted in his gut like
a dull blade.

"She's still my wife." The words came out in a hiss, bitter as
unripe fruit. His eyes narrowed as Marco's hand brushed Eliza's
shoulder, a casual touch that spoke of growing intimacy. Each
point of contact between them felt like a personal betrayal.

The camp they'd built together stood as a monument to his
irrelevance. Their little kingdom of survival skills and shared labor left no room for his expertise in hostile takeovers and market
manipulation. But Richard knew how to destroy things from
within - he'd built his fortune on that talent. He'd dismantled
entire corporations with less motivation than this.

He waited until they walked out of sight, then slipped into
the camp with practiced stealth. The fire pit Marco had con-

structed needed only minor adjustments - a few key stones removed here, support branches shifted there. When it collapsed,
it would look like simple bad construction. The water collection
system was even easier to sabotage - a small puncture in the leaf
they used to funnel rain would waste precious drinking water.
His fingers worked with surgical precision, each act of sabotage
carefully calculated.

"Eliza." He caught her alone later, his voice soft with practiced concern, honey-sweet and familiar. "You're looking tired.
Here, I saved you some coconut water." He pressed the shell into
her hands, noting how her guard dropped at this small kindness.
The old patterns were still there, waiting to be awakened.

"Thank you, Richard." Her smile, though hesitant, gave him
hope. He could still reach her, still remind her of their shared
history. The past wasn't dead - it just needed resurrection.

"Remember that resort in Bali? The way the sunset painted
the ocean just like this?" He gestured at the horizon, carefully recreating his charming persona from their courtship days.
"We had plans, Eliza. Dreams. This... situation... doesn't change
what we built together." His words were carefully chosen ar-
rows, aimed at her nostalgia.

He reached for her hand, but she pulled away, leaving him
grasping at empty air. The rejection stung, feeding his determination like fuel on a fire. She was his - his wife, his carefully
chosen partner, his most valuable acquisition. No shipwreck or
glorified cabin boy would rewrite that fundamental truth. He'd
invested too much to let her slip away.

Each time Marco and Eliza grew closer, Richard's sabotage became more focused, more precise. A missing tool here, a spoiled food cache there. Small things that bred frustration and doubt, hairline cracks that would eventually shatter their growing bond. He'd won Eliza once through careful strategy, orchestrating their courtship like a hostile takeover. He'd win her back the same way, one calculated move at a time.

———◆○◆———

Thunder cracked overhead as rain hammered the island. Marco hauled the last of their supplies into the cave while Eliza held a makeshift palm torch, illuminating the narrow entrance. Richard huddled in the back, his expensive shirt soaked through, water dripping from his perfectly styled hair onto his collar.

"Found something interesting." Marco pulled a bottle from his waterproof bag, muscles flexing with the careful movement. "Rescued it from the yacht's galley before we abandoned ship." The amber liquid sloshed inside the crystal decanter, catching the flickering torchlight.

"Macallan 25. At least something civilized survived." Richard reached for the bottle, his manicured fingers grasping at air as Marco pulled it back.

"We share equally here." Marco uncorked it, the rich aroma of aged scotch filling the confined space, momentarily overwhelming the dank smell of wet stone and earth.

Eliza pressed herself against the cave wall, acutely aware of both men's presence. The storm drove them deeper inside, until they formed a tight triangle in the cramped shelter. Lightning flashed, casting stark shadows across their faces, highlighting the tension in their jaw lines and the darkness in their eyes.

"To survival." Marco took a swig and passed the bottle to Eliza. The liquor burned down her throat, warming her rain-chilled body, leaving a trail of heat that settled in her stomach.

"To what we've lost." Richard's words carried a double meaning as he watched Eliza's lips touch the bottle where Marco's had been. His knuckles whitened against his soaked trousers.

The scotch circulated again, the bottle growing lighter with each pass. Thunder boomed, making Eliza jump. Her shoulder brushed Marco's chest, lingering longer than necessary, feeling the steady rhythm of his heartbeat. Richard's eyes narrowed at the contact, his breathing becoming shallow and controlled.

"Quite a change from your usual champagne parties, isn't it darling?" Richard's cultured voice had acquired an edge, sharp as broken glass.

"I don't miss them." Eliza met his gaze, defiance flickering in her eyes. "All those fake smiles and empty conversations."

"You used to excel at those empty conversations." He twisted the wedding ring on his finger.

"Maybe I'm tired of excelling at things that don't matter." Her voice was quiet but firm, like steel wrapped in silk.

Marco shifted, his leg pressing against Eliza's in the confined space. The air grew thick with unspoken words and suppressed desires, heavy as the storm clouds outside. Another flash of lightning illuminated the tension on their faces, casting harsh shadows that emphasized every line of frustration and want.

"This cave's getting crowded." Richard took another long pull from the bottle, drops of scotch clinging to his lower lip. "Almost as crowded as our marriage."

"Richard-" Eliza warned, her voice tight with anger and embarrassment.

"No, let's be honest for once. We're all trapped here anyway." He laughed without humor, the sound echoing off the cave walls like breaking glass. "Tell me, darling, when did you stop loving me? Before or after you started looking at him?"

Thunder crashed as Eliza's hand trembled around the bottle. "I haven't stopped loving you, Richard. I've just stopped pretending."

"Pretending what?" Richard's voice cracked like the lightning outside.

"That I'm happy being your trophy wife. Your perfect hostess. Your... acquisition." She spat the last word, years of resentment bubbling to the surface.

Marco moved to stand, but Richard shot forward, grabbing his collar. "Stay right there. You're part of this conversation too, aren't you? The noble savage, teaching my wife how to build fires and collect rainwater. Opening her eyes to a simpler life." His knuckles whitened against Marco's shirt.

"Let go." Marco's voice remained steady, but his muscles tensed beneath Richard's grip.

"Or what? You'll show me more of those survival skills? Demonstrate your superiority again?" Richard shoved him against the cave wall. "You think I don't see how you look at her?"

"Richard, stop!" Eliza grabbed his arm, but he shrugged her off.

"No, let him speak." Marco didn't resist, didn't fight back. "Tell us what really bothers you - that I look at her, or that she looks back?"

Richard's fist connected with Marco's jaw, the impact echoing through the cave. Blood trickled from Marco's split lip, but his eyes never left Richard's face.

"You had everything!" Richard's composed façade cracked completely. "The perfect life, the perfect wife, everything I gave you!" He whirled toward Eliza, his voice breaking. "And you threw it all away for him?"

"I didn't throw anything away." Eliza stepped between them, her voice steady despite her shaking hands. "This entire experience did that. But it also showed me who you really are - and who I've become while trying to be what you wanted."

Richard's face contorted, muscles twitching beneath his now bearded face. His eyes locked with Eliza's, searching for any trace of the polished socialite he'd married. Blood drained from his features as the truth of her words sank in, leaving his tanned skin ashen and sickly in the cave's dim light.

His mouth opened and closed, like a fish gasping on deck. The scotch bottle dangled from his fingers, amber liquid catching the dim light and casting dancing shadows on the limestone walls. The cave walls pressed in around them, amplifying the sound of their ragged breathing and the distant rumble of thunder.

"You are who you are, Liz." His voice cracked on her name, thick with bitterness and something that might have been grief. "And that will never change, no matter how many many fish you catch or how many berries you and your cabin boy here collect."

The bottle crashed against stone as he released it, the sharp sound making Marco flinch. Scotch pooled at their feet, mixing with rainwater and mud, its expensive aroma filling the humid air. Richard spun on his heel and lurched toward the cave entrance, his designer shoes slipping on the slick ground.

Lightning split the sky, illuminating his silhouette against sheets of rain that fell in silvery curtains. Wind howled through palm trees, bending them like desperate dancers, their fronds thrashing against the turbulent sky.

"Richard, wait!" Eliza stumbled forward, reaching out with one trembling hand. "It's not safe out there! The storm is getting worse!"

But he was already gone, swallowed by the storm's fury. Her voice echoed off empty stone, drowned by thunder that shook the very ground beneath their feet.

CHAPTER TWELVE

Natural Selection

Richard gripped the makeshift spear, its bamboo shaft smooth from six weeks of failed attempts. Sweat trickled down his neck despite the early morning chill. A set of fresh boar tracks cut through the mud ahead - his chance to finally prove himself. The prints were deep and wide, suggesting a large male, exactly the kind of quarry he'd been warned to avoid.

"I don't need their help." His expensive watch, now scratched and useless, caught the dawn light. "I ran a Fortune 500 company. I can handle a pig." The words sounded hollow even to his own ears, but he pushed the doubt aside.

The tracks led him deeper into the jungle's interior, past the markers Marco had established as safe zones. Thorny vines tore at his tattered Ralph Lauren shirt as he pushed through dense undergrowth. His designer shoes, reduced to worn soles held together with plant fiber, slipped on moss-covered rocks. The humid air grew thicker, carrying the pungent scent of rotting vegetation and something muskier - animal.

Blood spots dotted the ground - the boar was injured. Richard's pace quickened, his breath coming in sharp bursts. The terrain grew steeper, forcing him to scramble up loose scree slopes. Pride drove him forward. He'd show them he could adapt, could survive without their constant guidance. Six weeks of patronizing looks and whispered doubts would end today.

A grunt echoed through the trees. Richard froze, knuckles white around his spear. Twenty yards ahead, the wounded boar stood cornered against a rock face, tusks gleaming red. Its dark eyes fixed on him with primal fury. Steam rose from its heaving flanks in the cool morning air, and foam flecked its massive jaws.

"Just like closing a merger." Richard's voice quavered. He raised the spear, mimicking Marco's stance from previous hunts. His arms trembled with exhaustion and fear, betraying his false confidence.

The boar charged. Richard thrust the spear forward, but his foot slipped on loose stones. The weapon glanced off the animal's thick hide. Sharp pain exploded through his leg as the boar's tusk ripped flesh. His scream echoed across the valley as he tumbled backward, the world becoming a blur of green and brown.

Rock met skull with a sickening crack. The world spun. When it settled, Richard found himself wedged in a narrow crevice, his leg bent at an impossible angle. Blood ran warm down his face. Above, the jungle canopy swayed like a distant green sea. The pain was overwhelming, each breath sending new waves of agony through his broken body.

"Help!" His voice came out weak, barely carrying past the rock walls that imprisoned him. "Please... somebody..." The words dissolved into quiet sobs as reality set in. He could hear the boar's heavy breathing somewhere above, waiting.

Pride dissolved into raw fear as shadows lengthened across his trapped form. The corporate titan who once commanded boardrooms now lay broken, nature's harsh lesson in humility carved into his flesh. Each passing minute brought new under-standing of his foolishness, but wisdom had come at a terrible price.

Marco emerged from the surf, fish speared for breakfast dan-gling from his belt. His keen eyes swept the beach camp, noting the missing spear and disturbed sand leading toward the jun-gle. The morning sun cast long shadows across their makeshift settlement, highlighting the telltale signs of someone's hasty departure.

"Where's Richard?" He dropped the fish by the smoking fire where Eliza sorted through medicinal plants. Dew still clung to the leaves she'd gathered, her fingers stained green from her work.

"Haven't seen him since dawn." She shielded her eyes, scan-ning the tree line. "I thought he was gathering wood." Worry creased her weathered face as she stood, brushing sand from her worn clothes.

Marco's jaw tightened as he spotted broken branches past their safety markers. "He went hunting alone." Without another word, he grabbed his own spear and tracking kit, the leather pouch worn smooth from months of daily use.

The trail wasn't hard to follow - Richard had crashed through the undergrowth like a wounded animal, leaving torn vegetation and scattered stones in his wake. Marco moved swiftly but cautiously, reading the signs of the hunt gone wrong: blood spatter, scattered leaves, the deep gouges of boar tusks in tree bark. The morning mist still clung to the forest floor, carrying the metallic scent of fresh blood.

"Richard!" His call echoed through the canopy. A weak moan answered from below, followed by the sound of loose stones skittering down rock.

Marco peered over a rocky ledge. Twenty feet down, wedged in a narrow crevice, Richard lay broken and bleeding. Above him, the wounded boar paced, its dark bristles matted with blood and foam, waiting for its prey to weaken further. Steam rose from its heaving flanks in the cool morning air.

"Don't move." Marco's voice carried quiet authority. He circled wide, positioning himself between the boar and its intended victim. The animal charged, hooves thundering against the earth. Marco pivoted, his spear finding its mark behind the shoulder blade. The boar crashed down, its final breath rattling through bloody foam, massive body twitching before going still.

Getting Richard out required all of Marco's strength. He fashioned a harness from vines, bracing himself against the rock face as he hauled the injured man up inch by agonizing inch. Richard's designer clothes, now shredded and filthy, caught on sharp stones. His whimpers of pain turned to sobs of humiliation. Sweat soaked through Marco's shirt as he worked, muscles straining against the dead weight.

"I could have handled it," Richard gasped as Marco laid him on level ground. Blood matted his silver hair, and his leg bent at an unnatural angle. His once-commanding voice now trembled with shock and pain.

Marco's expression remained neutral as he began splinting the broken limb with practiced movements. "No. You couldn't." The simple statement carried more weight than any lecture. In those three words, months of corporate hierarchy crumbled. Nature had rendered its final verdict on their relative worth, and no corner office could change its ruling.

Eliza dabbed Richard's forehead with a damp cloth woven from shredded clothing. Her touch lingered, gentle yet precise, as she cleaned dried blood from the gash above his temple. The morning sun filtered through their shelter's palm fronds, casting dappled shadows across his ashen face. The makeshift bandages they'd crafted lay in neat rolls beside her, each one a testament to their growing resourcefulness.

"The fever's getting worse." She pressed cool leaves against his skin, their medicinal oils releasing a sharp, minty scent. Her fingers traced the edge of the wound, noting the angry red streaks spreading outward. Sweat beaded on his brow despite the morning chill, and his breathing came in shallow gasps.

Marco ducked through the shelter's entrance, arms laden with fresh bamboo and vine cordage. "Found more of those antibiotic leaves you wanted." He set down a bundle of dark green foliage beside her. "And some wild ginger for the pain." His foraging skills had become invaluable, each trip into the jungle yielding new medicines and materials.

Richard stirred, his eyes focusing on Marco with newfound clarity. Gone was the condescending glare of the corporate executive. In its place, raw gratitude shone through the haze of fever. His hands trembled as they clutched at the woven mat beneath him.

"I should have listened." Richard's voice cracked. Each word seemed to cost him tremendous effort. "All those weeks... teaching us... I was too proud." His admission hung in the humid air, heavy with regret and recognition.

Eliza's hands stilled as she wrung out the cloth. The intimacy of caring for him had stripped away their previous roles - socialite, businessman, crew member. Here, skill and wisdom marked the true hierarchy. She noticed how his manicured nails had grown ragged, how his designer watch now lay discarded in a corner.

"Hold still." She lifted his head, supporting his neck as Marco pressed a cup of bitter tea to his lips. Richard drank without complaint, accepting their care with a humility that would have been unthinkable six weeks ago. The pungent brew stained his cracked lips.

"The leg needs to be rewrapped." Marco gathered fresh leaves and bandages. His movements were swift, practiced, born of necessity and experience. Richard tensed but didn't protest as they worked together to tend his wounds. The splint they'd fashioned held firm, though the skin around it had turned mottled and bruised.

"Thank you." Richard's whisper carried the weight of transformation. "Both of you." His hand found Eliza's, squeezing weakly. The gesture acknowledged more than gratitude - it was a surrender of power, an acceptance of their new reality. Tears gathered in the corners of his eyes, whether from pain or emotion, none could say.

The morning breeze carried salt spray through their shelter, mixing with the herbal scents of healing. In this moment of vulnerability, the last vestiges of their old social order dissolved like footprints in the tide. Birds called from the jungle canopy, indifferent to the human drama unfolding beneath their perches.

Weeks passed as Richard's leg healed. He sat by the signal fire, feeding small branches into the flames while Marco demonstrated proper knot-tying techniques to Eliza. The hierarchy had settled into an unspoken rhythm - Marco led, Richard followed, and Eliza bridged the gap between them.

"The bowline needs to be tighter." Marco adjusted Eliza's grip on the rope, his weathered hands guiding hers with practiced ease. "See how it holds now? This could save your life one day."

Richard watched their easy rapport, no longer bristling at Marco's authority. His own rope lay in his lap, fingers working the knots with careful attention. The calluses on his hands marked his transformation from CEO to student. The rope's rough fibers, once foreign to his manicured hands, now felt familiar and essential.

"Richard, show me your progress." Marco's tone carried neither mockery nor challenge - just the steady assurance of a leader who knew his role. The morning sun cast long shadows across their makeshift classroom.

Richard held up his work without hesitation, squinting at his handiwork. "I think I've got it, but the third loop keeps slipping. The angle isn't quite right."

"Here." Eliza took the rope, demonstrating the correction with fluid movements. "Marco showed me a trick - think of it like threading a needle." Her gentle guidance smoothed the interaction, preserving Richard's dignity while reinforcing Marco's expertise. The rope danced through her fingers, forming perfect loops.

"The tide's turning." Marco gathered his fishing gear, testing the point of his handcrafted spear. "Richard, mind the fire. Eliza, those palm fronds need replacing before the next storm. The last rain nearly flooded the shelter."

"Of course." They answered in unison, accepting the tasks without question. The response would have been unthinkable months ago, when Richard barked orders and Eliza deferred to social status. Now their voices carried equal measures of respect and purpose.

As Marco headed toward the surf, Richard adjusted his position by the fire, massaging his healing leg. "He's right about the weather. I can feel it in my leg." The admission came easily now, free of resentment or pride. Dark clouds gathered on the horizon, confirming his prediction.

"We've all changed." Eliza paused in her work, looking between the two men, her hands full of fresh palm fronds. "For the better, I think. We're stronger together than we ever were apart."

Richard nodded, his attention already returning to the knots in his lap, fingers moving with growing confidence. The old power dynamics had washed away like footprints in the sand, replaced by something more practical, more real. In their place, a new order had emerged - one based not on wealth or status, but on capability and mutual respect. The island had stripped away their pretenses, leaving only their true selves behind.

CHAPTER THIRTEEN

Paradise and Prison

Two months had carved new patterns into their lives, as natural as the tides. Eliza woke before sunrise, her body no longer craving silk sheets or air conditioning. The bamboo platform she shared with Marco felt more like home than her penthouse ever had, the gentle creak of wood beneath them a familiar lullaby each night.

She watched Marco check the fish traps, his movements precise and purposeful, a dance learned through necessity and perfected through devotion. The morning light caught the silver streaks in his dark hair, earned from years at sea. A gentle breeze carried the salt spray as her heart quickened when he turned to wave, his smile genuine and warm.

"Breakfast?" She held up two ripe papayas from their grove, their sweet scent mingling with the ocean air.

"Perfect timing." He joined her at their cooking area, a well-organized space with stone tools and woven baskets, each item carefully placed and maintained. Their hands brushed as she passed him a slice of fruit, skin sun-bronzed and weathered. The touch lingered, electric with unspoken meaning, a language they'd developed in shared glances and careful touches.

Richard sat apart, scribbling calculations in his weathered notebook, his Harvard education seemingly at odds with their primitive surroundings. "The trade winds shift next month. Our chances of rescue increase by forty percent." His pen scratched against the paper with desperate precision.

Eliza barely heard him. She watched Marco demonstrate a new way to weave palm fronds, his hands guiding hers through the motions, each twist and turn creating something beautiful from nothing. Their shelter had evolved into a comfortable home, with raised sleeping platforms, storage areas, and even a small garden where herbs and wild island vegetables thrived in the fertile soil.

"We could expand the north wall," Marco suggested, his shoulder pressed against hers, warm and solid. "Add more space for storing dried fish."

"And maybe a proper table?" Eliza smiled, already planning the improvement, imagining shared meals and quiet evenings. The idea of permanence no longer frightened her, instead filling her with a quiet contentment.

She glanced at her bare wrist where her diamond watch had once sat, worth more than most people earned in a year. The tan line had faded, along with her attachment to such trinkets. Here, time flowed like water, measured in sunrises and moon phases rather than business meetings and social obligations, each day rich with purpose and meaning.

Richard's voice cut through her thoughts, sharp and insistent. "Once we're back, we'll need to restructure the company's Pacific operations."

Eliza caught Marco's eye and saw her own truth reflected there, in depths as clear and honest as the lagoon at dawn. The thought of returning to board rooms and charity galas felt hollow compared to the authentic life they'd built, stripped of pretense and filled with genuine connection. Her fingers intertwined with Marco's, rough with calluses, strong from honest work, telling a story of transformation. In losing everything, she'd found what mattered - a truth as simple and profound as the rhythm of the waves against their shore.

Eliza stirred the pot of fish stew, breathing in the aromatic blend of wild herbs and coconut. Their kitchen area had evolved from a simple fire pit to an organized space with stone counters and bamboo utensil holders. Marco's influence showed in every practical detail, from the way the cooking implements hung within easy reach to the clever drainage system he'd built for washing. The shelves he'd crafted held their collection of dried spices in repurposed glass jars, each one labeled in his precise handwriting.

Marco stepped behind her, his chest pressed against her back as he reached around to drop fresh-cut chili into the pot. His breath tickled her neck, and she leaned into his warmth, their bodies fitting together with practiced ease. The familiar scent of sea salt and sunshine clung to his skin.

"Smells good." His lips brushed her ear. "Better than any five-star restaurant."

She turned in his arms, tasting salt on his skin as she kissed his shoulder. "Give me fresh-caught tuna any day." The memory of overpriced fusion cuisine in sterile restaurants seemed almost comical now.

Their evening routine flowed like a dance - Marco straining coconut milk while Eliza tended the fire, their movements synchronized without need for words. They'd created their own version of domestic bliss, far removed from the sterile luxury of her former life. The rhythmic sound of waves provided their dinner music, more soothing than any carefully curated playlist.

Yet as she ladled stew into wooden bowls, a familiar restlessness stirred. The sunset painted the sky in brilliant oranges and pinks, but her eyes drifted to the horizon. Something tugged at her, even as Marco's hand found the small of her back, even as their home wrapped around them in cozy simplicity. The mainland's pull was subtle but persistent, like a tide she couldn't quite ignore.

They settled on their woven mat, shoulders touching, feet tangled together. Marco fed her a piece of mango, juice running down his fingers. She caught his hand, kissed each callused fingertip, savoring the intimacy of the moment. His eyes darkened with desire, reflecting the flickering firelight. The fruit's sweetness lingered on her tongue, a reminder of nature's simple pleasures.

The breeze carried night-blooming jasmine from their garden, mixing with the smoke from their cooking fire. Their primitive paradise held everything they needed - each other, sustenance, shelter. But in quiet moments like these, questions whispered through Eliza's mind like the wind through palm fronds, unsettling her hard-won peace. The weight of unspoken decisions hung in the air between bites of stew and tender touches.

Eliza wandered the beach at low tide, scanning the wet sand for treasures revealed by the retreating waves. A flash of iridescent pink caught her eye - a perfect conch shell, polished smooth by the sea. She picked it up, turning it over in her hands. The shell's pearly interior reflected her face, and her breath caught.

A stranger stared back. Sun-bleached streaks painted her once-carefully maintained dark hair. Her skin, despite Marco's ingenious coconut oil moisturizer, had weathered into leather. Lines etched around her eyes from squinting at the sun sparkled with a map of tiny freckles across her nose and cheeks. Even her posture had changed - the rigid corporate stance replaced by something more fluid, more primal.

She traced the rough patches on her palms, remembering weekly manicures at Bella's on Fifth Avenue. The scent of acetone and lavender lotion. The gossip magazines. The champagne they served in delicate flutes while her cuticles were trimmed and shaped. The way Sandra, her favorite technician, would tsk at the smallest chip in her perfect gel overlay.

Her knees hit the sand. The weekly routine flashed through her mind - Brazilian blowouts, microdermabrasion, yoga with Catherine, lunch at Le Bernardin. Shopping trips to Paris for the season's collections. The weight of silk against her skin, the whisper of cashmere, the click of Louboutin heels on marble floors. The endless meetings with investors, the power suits.

Tears splashed onto the shell's surface, distorting her reflection. She'd adapted to island life, learned to survive, even found love. But this moment of clarity struck deep - she barely recognized herself. The polished trophy wife who had led a life of luxury and opulence had vanished, replaced by this wild creature with tangled hair and sun-roughened skin. Her once-manicured nails now bore the honest dirt of garden work and fishing.

Her fingers clutched the shell tighter. The cost of survival meant sacrificing every comfort she'd known. No hot showers. No climate control. No Egyptian cotton sheets or memory foam mattresses. No restaurants or theater nights or gallery openings. No more mindless scrolling through social media feeds or midnight food deliveries. The constant hum of technology had been replaced by cricket songs and ocean waves.

The weight of civilization's absence crushed her chest. She'd traded everything - her carefully curated life, her meticulously maintained appearance, her position at the top of society's ladder - for the raw authenticity of survival. The question that had lurked beneath the surface finally emerged: Had the trade been worth it? Was this simpler existence, despite its hardships, somehow more real than the artificial perfection she'd left behind?

The shell slipped from her trembling fingers, landing with a soft thud in the sand. Her reflection shattered into fragments of pearl and shadow, like pieces of her former self scattered across the shore.

Richard emerged from the jungle's edge, his shirt stained with juice, holding something wrapped in broad leaves. His designer watch, though scratched and weathered, still caught the sunlight - a reminder of their shared world of wealth and privilege. Even here, the Patek Philippe's gleam spoke of board rooms and billion-dollar deals.

"Found these growing on the north ridge." He unwrapped the bundle, revealing perfectly ripe mountain apples, their red skin gleaming. "Remember that orchard at our Hampton house? The ones you'd pick every summer?"

Eliza's fingers brushed the smooth fruit. "The trees you imported from Japan. Twenty thousand dollars each." The memory of signing that check felt absurd now, after months of scrounging for basic sustenance.

"Worth every penny to see you happy." Richard settled beside her on the driftwood log, his movements still carrying that practiced grace of old money. "Those garden parties you threw. The way you transformed our home into something magical."

Her throat tightened at the memory of crystal champagne flutes catching sunset light, of string quartets playing across manicured lawns. "That feels like another life." Another version of herself, perfectly coiffed and supremely confident.

"It can be our life again." His hand found hers, familiar yet strange after months of separation. The calluses on his once-manicured fingers felt foreign. "When we're rescued, I'll rebuild everything. Better than before. The penthouse in Manhattan, winters in St. Barts, your charity foundation."

The fruit's sweetness burst across her tongue, transporting her to climate-controlled rooms and silk sheets. "I've changed, Richard." The words came out barely above a whisper.

"We all have. But some things remain constant." He pulled a small piece of paper from his pocket - a crumpled photo of them at their wedding, her in Vera Wang, him in Tom Ford. The edges were worn smooth from frequent handling. "Our connection. Our understanding of that world. Marco... he can't give you what I can."

The truth of his words settled like lead in her stomach. Marco's love was pure, untainted by wealth or status. But Richard offered security, a return to everything she'd spent a lifetime building. The fruit's juice ran down her chin as she wrestled with desires she thought she'd buried - the yearning for simple luxuries like hot showers and fresh coffee, the comfort of knowing tomorrow was guaranteed by money in the bank. Each sweet bite seemed to pull her back toward that gilded existence.

"Just think about it," Richard whispered, his voice carrying the weight of their shared history and the promise of restored privilege. The sea breeze carried away his words, but their impact remained, heavy and insistent.

Moonlight filtered through the woven palm roof, casting latticed shadows across Marco's sleeping form. Eliza traced them with her eyes, following the patterns down his weathered face, past the small scar above his eyebrow from a fishing accident last spring. His chest rose and fell with the rhythm of the waves outside, peaceful and steady. No pretense, no hidden agendas - just pure, honest existence.

Richard's words from earlier echoed in her mind, persistent as the tide. He slept in his separate shelter, probably dreaming of spreadsheets and stock options. Even here, stripped of wealth, he clung to the structures of their old life like a lifeline.

She shifted on the bamboo platform, careful not to wake Marco, mindful of the creaking spots she'd learned to avoid. His arm lay across her waist, protective even in sleep. Those hands had taught her to fish, to weave, to survive, their roughness a testament to honest work. Richard's hands had only ever signed checks, manicured and soft from a lifetime of boardrooms.

The night air carried salt and jasmine through their shelter, mingling with the earthier scent of smoke from the evening's cooking fire. Here, she answered to no one. No charity board meetings, no social obligations, no carefully maintained image to uphold. She'd traded Chanel suits for hand-woven palm skirts, found strength in calluses instead of credit cards.

Marco stirred, mumbling something in his native tongue, a language she was slowly beginning to understand. His face pressed against her shoulder, trusting and vulnerable. With him, every touch felt real, earned through shared struggle and genuine connection. Richard's touches had always carried the weight of social contract, of merger and acquisition, each gesture calculated and proper.

But Richard understood her other hungers - for art, for culture, for the rush of closing million-dollar deals. He knew the woman she'd spent decades becoming, could speak of Beethoven and Bordeaux, not just the survivor she'd been forced to become.

Eliza stared at the moon through gaps in the roof, counting the stars that peeked through the spaces between leaves. For the first time, she consciously listed her options: Stay, embrace this simpler life with Marco, find meaning in daily survival and honest love. Or return with Richard, reclaim her power in the corporate world, satisfy her ambitions. Each path would cost her something precious. Each would grant her something essential.

Her fingers found Marco's heartbeat, strong and steady against her palm, its rhythm somehow more honest than any Swiss watch she'd ever owned. The choice loomed before her like storm clouds on the horizon, impossible to ignore any longer, demanding resolution before dawn broke over the island.

CHAPTER FOURTEEN

Dreams of the Future

The morning sun painted the beach in amber hues as Eliza traced patterns in the sand with a broken shell, her fingers leaving delicate swirls that would soon be washed away by the tide. Marco sat beside her, their shoulders touching, both watching the waves lap at the shore, the salty breeze carrying memories of their shared ordeal.

"You know what's funny?" Marco stretched his legs out toward the water, his weathered boat shoes collecting tiny grains of sand. "Before all this, I dreamed of owning my own boat. Something similar to the vessels I worked on. Maybe a sixty-footer with classic lines."

"What stopped you?"

"Money. Connections." His fingers brushed against hers in the sand, rough calluses meeting soft skin. "But this experience.

.. it taught me something. Those wealthy tourists who chartered the Aurora? They paid thousands for manufactured adventure. What if we offered them the real thing?"

Eliza turned to face him, intrigued, tucking a strand of wind-blown hair behind her ear. "What do you mean?"

"A charter company, but different. Teaching survival skills, real seamanship. Not just serving cocktails and pointing out dolphins." His eyes lit up as he spoke, the same intensity she'd seen when he'd guided them through their darkest moments. "Rich folks pay big money to climb Everest, to test themselves. Why not combine luxury with actual adventure?"

"Survival training for the wealthy?" Eliza's business mind kicked in, years of experience watching Richard wheel and deal with his wealthy clientele at countless yacht club gatherings and marina events. "That's... brilliant actually. They'd pay premium rates for authenticity."

"You understand their world, I understand the sea and survival. Together..." He left the sentence hanging, his gaze fixed on the horizon where sky met ocean.

"We'd need capital to start. Boats aren't cheap." She absently rubbed her thumb over the shell's smooth surface.

"I've got savings. Not much, but enough for a down payment on a decent vessel." Marco picked up a piece of driftwood, sketching boat designs in the sand, adding details of cabin layouts and deck spaces. "With your connections and my practical knowledge..."

"We could create something unique." Eliza's heart raced at the possibility, her mind already mapping out marketing strategies and client lists. "Combine luxury with real adventure. Teaching actual skills instead of just pampering people."

"Exactly." Marco's hand found hers, warm and steady against her palm. "No more working for others. Building something real, together, something for us. Something that matters."

The waves crashed against the shore as they sat together, sharing ideas, building castles not of sand but of possibility. Seabirds wheeled overhead as they discussed logistics, equipment needs, and training programs. The morning sun climbed higher, warming their skin as they planned their future, one that bridged both their worlds, transforming their shared trauma into something meaningful and new.

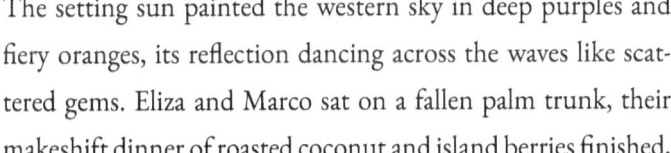

The setting sun painted the western sky in deep purples and fiery oranges, its reflection dancing across the waves like scattered gems. Eliza and Marco sat on a fallen palm trunk, their makeshift dinner of roasted coconut and island berries finished, empty shells scattered at their feet.

"So, Captain Marco..." Eliza bumped his shoulder with hers, breathing in the salt-tinged evening air. "Will you make all your clients scale palm trees for coconuts, or just the special ones?"

"Only the pretty ones." His eyes crinkled at the corners, the fading sunlight catching the gold flecks in his irises. "Though I might need to demonstrate the proper technique first."

"Oh, I see how it is. Using your survival skills to show off." She traced her finger along a groove in the bark, feeling its weathered texture. "And what about those fancy yachties who can't tell port from starboard?"

"They'll learn. Or swim."

"Harsh teacher." She grinned, watching the sun sink lower into the horizon's embrace. "But I bet they'll love it. Especially when you do that thing where you navigate by the stars."

"What thing?"

"You know, when you get all serious and point at the sky, explaining celestial navigation. Your eyes light up like the constellations themselves." Her voice carried a gentle teasing note, but her words held genuine warmth.

Marco's hand found hers on the trunk, his calloused fingers familiar against her skin. "Speaking of navigation... where do you see yourself in this venture? Besides handling the business side?"

"Well..." She leaned closer, her voice dropping to a playful whisper that matched the evening's hushed atmosphere. "I thought I might learn a few tricks from this rugged sailor I know. Maybe even become a captain myself one day."

"Is that so?"

"Mhmm. Though I might need some private lessons. Lots of them." Her fingers intertwined with his, fitting perfectly between the spaces. "And someone to show me the ropes... literally."

"That could be arranged." His thumb traced circles on her palm, sending tiny shivers up her arm. "Though I warn you, I am very thorough with my teaching methods."

"Good." Eliza rested her head on his shoulder, watching the last sliver of the sun disappear beneath the watery horizon. "Because I plan to master every aspect of this business. The sailing, the survival skills..." She tilted her face toward his, close enough to feel the warmth of his breath. "And especially the captain."

Dawn broke over the island, painting the sky in watercolor streaks of pink and gold. Eliza stood ankle-deep in the crystalline shallows, her borrowed knife poised above the water's surface. Marco's bare feet shifted in the sand behind her, his chest pressed against her back as he guided her stance, the warmth of his skin seeping through her thin shirt.

"Keep your shadow behind you," he whispered, his hands adjusting her shoulders with gentle pressure. "Fish can't see up well, but they spot movement above them. The slightest ripple can scatter them."

"Like this?" She adjusted her position, feeling the water's gentle push against her legs, focusing on staying perfectly still despite her racing heart.

"Perfect. Now wait..." His breath tickled her ear, sending a pleasant shiver down her spine. "There—strike!"

The knife plunged into the water. A silver flash, a splash, and a small fish flopped on the beach, scales glinting in the early morning light.

"I did it!" Eliza dropped the knife and wrapped her arms around Marco's neck, her wet feet leaving prints in the sand as she spun to face him. "First try!"

"Natural talent." He squeezed her waist, pride evident in his dark eyes. "Now for the hard part—cleaning it."

They moved to a flat rock where Marco demonstrated the precise cuts needed to fillet their catch, his experienced hands moving with practiced efficiency. Eliza's hands trembled as she copied his movements, but her determination showed in the furrow of her brow and the set of her jaw. The salty breeze carried the fresh scent of the sea around them.

"Your turn to teach me something," Marco said as they finished preparing the fish, wiping his hands on a scrap of cloth.

"What could I possibly—"

"Those berries you found yesterday. Show me how you knew they were safe."

Eliza led him to the forest's edge, pushing aside broad leaves still heavy with morning dew as she pointed out the distinctive leaf patterns and growth habits she'd observed. "See how the birds eat these? And the color—nature warns you about poison with bright reds and yellows. These purple ones are safe."

"Smart girl." Marco plucked a berry, rolling it between his fingers thoughtfully. "What else?"

"The stems have these tiny hairs, and the leaves grow in pairs." She demonstrated, running her finger along the plant, her scholarly enthusiasm showing through. "I watched which fruits the local birds ate, then tested just one berry first. Waited hours before trying more."

"Resourceful and cautious." His hand found the small of her back, thumb tracing small circles there. "You're a quick study."

They spent the morning foraging and practicing knots with vines, their laughter echoing across the beach as they challenged each other to increasingly complex tasks. Marco taught her a sailor's knot that could be released with a single pull, while she showed him how to weave palm fronds into a simple basket. Every touch lingered, every shared glance held meaning, their partnership growing stronger with each passing moment under the warming tropical sun.

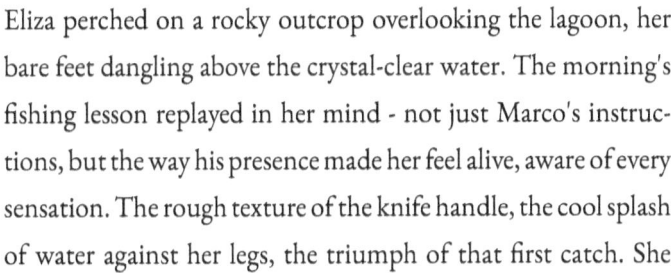

Eliza perched on a rocky outcrop overlooking the lagoon, her bare feet dangling above the crystal-clear water. The morning's fishing lesson replayed in her mind - not just Marco's instructions, but the way his presence made her feel alive, aware of every sensation. The rough texture of the knife handle, the cool splash of water against her legs, the triumph of that first catch. She could still feel the proud squeeze of his hand on her shoulder when she'd landed it.

Her old life seemed distant now, filled with endless meetings and artificial pleasures. She'd spent years chasing status symbols - the right clothes, the perfect apartment, vacations that looked good on social media. But here, wearing borrowed clothes and living off the land, she felt more genuine than ever. The salt air had stripped away her carefully constructed façade, leaving something raw and real beneath.

"What are you thinking about?" Marco's voice carried from below as he collected driftwood along the shore, his tanned arms glistening with sea spray.

"How different everything feels now." She watched him work, admiring the fluid efficiency of his movements. "Back home, I measured success in dollar signs and LinkedIn connections. Here... it's about what your hands can create, what your mind can solve. What you can build from nothing but determination and skill."

Marco paused his gathering, shielding his eyes to look up at her. "And which do you prefer?"

"This." The answer came without hesitation. "Working with you, learning real skills, feeling the sun on my face... it's like I've been sleeping my whole life and finally woke up. Like everything before was just preparation for this moment."

She stretched her arms overhead, embracing the warmth of the tropical morning. Every muscle ached from their activities, but it was a good ache - the kind that meant growth, achievement. Marco had shown her strength she never knew she possessed, capabilities that lay dormant beneath designer suits and boardroom presentations. Each day brought new discoveries about herself, unlocked by his patient guidance and unwavering faith in her abilities.

"You make me believe in myself," she said softly, more to herself than to him. "Not just survive, but thrive. Build something meaningful." The business plan they'd discussed wasn't just about profits - it was about sharing this awakening with others, showing them what she'd discovered about herself through his eyes. About finding purpose in the simple act of creation, of self-reliance tempered with partnership.

The gentle lap of waves against the shore matched the rhythm of her heart as she watched him return to his task, each piece of wood he gathered was another building block in their shared vision. The morning light caught his movements, casting him in gold, and she smiled at how natural he looked here - as if he'd sprung fully formed from the island itself, a teacher she never knew she needed until fate intervened.

The campfire's flames danced between them, casting flickering shadows across their faces as night settled over the island. Marco added another piece of driftwood, sending sparks spiraling up toward the star-filled sky, the salt-crusted wood crackling and popping as it caught.

"I used to hate the ocean." His voice was soft, barely audible above the crackling fire. "When I was eight, my father's fishing boat went down in a storm. They never found him. Not even a piece of the hull washed ashore."

Eliza reached across the flames, her fingers finding his hand, feeling the rough calluses that spoke of years of hard work. "What changed?"

"I realized I needed to understand it. Master it. Spent every moment I could learning about the sea, about boats, about survival." His thumb traced patterns on her palm, gentle circles that matched the rhythm of the waves. "The ocean took my father, but it also gave me purpose. Taught me respect for forces bigger than myself."

"I get that. Finding meaning in loss." She drew her knees to her chest, watching the fire paint gold across his features, highlighting the quiet strength in his expression. "My mother had a drinking problem. She really wasn't there much for me and my sister. I threw myself into building the perfect life, thinking if I could just control everything..." She shook her head, remembering the endless meetings and empty achievements. "But it was all surface. No depth. Like trying to hold water in cupped hands."

"Until now?"

"Until you." Her voice caught, thick with emotion. "You showed me what real strength looks like. Not power suits and corner offices, but this." She gestured between them. "Trust. Vulnerability. Building something true. Something that matters."

Marco shifted closer, their shoulders touching, his warmth seeping through her thin shirt. "You know what scared me most about being a crew member? Not the storms or the work. It was watching wealthy people chase hollow dreams, thinking that's all there was to life. Seeing them trapped in gilded cages of their own making."

"And now?"

"Now I've found someone who sees beyond that. Who understands the value of real connection." His fingers interlaced with hers, strong and sure. "Someone who makes me want to build more than just a business. Someone who makes every sunrise feel like a gift."

The fire crackled between them, its warmth nothing compared to the heat in their shared gaze. Eliza leaned into him, feeling the steady rhythm of his heartbeat against her cheek, matching the distant pulse of waves on the shore.

"I'm not afraid anymore," she whispered, breathing in his scent of salt and cedar. "Not of the ocean, not of failing. Not of feeling this much."

Marco's arm wrapped around her shoulders, pulling her closer until there was no space left between them. "Neither am I."

CHAPTER FIFTEEN

The Lagoons Call

Moonlight painted silver paths across the lagoon's surface. The day's heat lingered in the air, making the cool water all the more inviting. Marco stood at the water's edge, his bare feet sinking into the soft sand, feeling the gentle pulse of tiny waves against his toes.

"Perfect temperature." He dipped his hand in the crystalline water, letting it run through his fingers. "After all that hiking, this is exactly what we need."

Eliza hung back, tugging at the hem of her salt-stained blouse, her eyes darting between the dark water and the safety of solid ground. "I don't know..."

"Trust me." As he began removing his pants Marco waded in up to his knees, tiny rivulets streaming down his calves. "The phosphorescence is incredible on nights like this."

As if to prove his point, each ripple around his legs sparked with tiny blue-green lights, like underwater fireflies dancing in his wake. Eliza stepped closer, mesmerized by the ethereal display, her earlier hesitation beginning to fade.

"It's like stars in the water." She crouched down, trailing her fingers through the surface. Light danced around her hand, trailing behind her movements in glowing ribbons, creating constellations that dissolved as quickly as they formed.

Marco splashed deeper into the lagoon, sending cascades of luminescence in every direction. "Come on. When else will you get to swim in liquid starlight?"

The moon caught the planes of his shoulders as he pulled his shirt over his head, water droplets gleaming on his skin. Eliza's breath caught. She glanced around the deserted beach, palm trees swaying gently in the evening breeze, then slowly began removing her clothes.

The water welcomed her like silk against her skin, cool but not cold, perfect for a night swim. Each movement created new patterns of light, surrounding them in a private galaxy of swirling blues and greens. Marco floated nearby, his smile visible in the moonlight, drops of water glistening in his hair.

"Worth it?"

"It's magical." Eliza spun in a slow circle, watching the light swirl around her like a luminous dress. The worries of survival, of rescue, of their uncertain future melted away in this moment of pure wonder, replaced by childlike amazement at nature's light show.

Marco swam closer, his movements creating interweaving patterns with hers, their personal light show growing more intricate with each passing moment. "You know what else is magical?"

"What?"

"The way you've changed since we got here. Like you've shed a shell you didn't even know you were wearing. You're more alive now, more free."

Their glowing trails merged as they drifted together in the gentle current, creating a spiral of light that slowly expanded outward. The air hummed with possibility, with unspoken words that floated between them like the bioluminescent creatures in the water, each glance and smile carrying weight in the ethereal atmosphere.

The phosphorescence swirled around them as Marco's hand found the small of her back, drawing her closer. Their luminous trails merged into one glowing pattern beneath the surface. Eliza's heart raced as his fingers traced up her spine, leaving trails of fire in their wake that had nothing to do with the water's light show.

"I crave you more and more each and every day, Eliza I can't get enough of you" Marco whispered, his breath warm against her ear. The moonlight silvered his features, catching droplets of water that clung to his long eyelashes.

Eliza's fingers traced the curve of his shoulder, marveling at how natural this felt, how right. "Me too."

Their lips met softly at first, tentative, exploring. The kiss deepened as Marco pulled her closer, their bodies pressed together in the warm water. Each movement created new patterns of light around them, as if the sea itself celebrated their connection.

"You're trembling." Marco's voice was husky as he brushed wet strands of hair from her face.

"Good trembling." She smiled against his lips, tasting salt water and something uniquely him. Her fingers tangled in his hair as she pulled him down for another kiss, more urgent this time.

They floated together, suspended in their private galaxy of bioluminescent stars, trading kisses that grew increasingly passionate. Marco's hands roamed her back, her shoulders, treating each inch of exposed skin like a treasure to be mapped and memorized.

"You are so beautiful," he murmured between kisses, his words punctuated by the soft splash of water. The moonlight caught the curve of her neck as she tilted her head back, his lips finding the sensitive spot just below her ear.

Eliza sighed, her body melting against his as their kisses grew deeper, more intense. The water lapped gently around them, creating endless patterns of light that mirrored the sparks flying between them. In this moment, the world beyond their luminous cocoon ceased to exist - there was only Marco, only the press of his body against hers, only the taste of his kisses and the sound of their mingled breath in the night air.

The lagoon's surface whispered secrets in a language of ripples and light, as Marco and Eliza's bodies moved in a dance as old as time. The water embraced them, a silken caress against their heated skin, the bioluminescence casting an otherworldly glow that enveloped them in its mystical shroud.

Eliza's fingers dug into Marco's shoulders, her breath coming in short gasps that mingled with the sound of the lapping water. His hands explored her with an urgency born of desperation and longing, each touch stoking the fire that blazed between them.

In the shelter of the lagoon, with the moon as their silent witness, they came together with a passion that was both a discovery and a homecoming. The world around them faded into insignificance as they surrendered to the powerful undertow of their desire.

Marco's whispered words of adoration and wonder were lost in the gentle splash of water and the pounding of Eliza's heart in her ears. Her response was wordless, a melody of gasps and sighs that harmonized with the rhythm of their lovemaking.

The bioluminescent organisms in the water responded to their movements, igniting in bursts of brilliant light that spiraled around them, casting an ethereal radiance on their union. It was as if the lagoon itself rejoiced in their connection, a physical manifestation of the bond that had been forged through shared hardship and a newfound respect and admiration.

As they reached the crescendo of their passion, their cries of ecstasy were swallowed by the vastness of the lagoon and the night, a testament to the raw and powerful forces that had brought them to this moment. The water that held them seemed to pulse with their release, sending out waves of luminescence that painted the dark with a fleeting but breathtaking display of natural fireworks.

In the aftermath, they floated together, their breaths gradually slowing, their hearts syncing with the gentle rhythm of the waves. The glow of the water gradually faded, but the light within each of them remained, a beacon of hope and connection that neither the unpredictable sea nor the unknown future could extinguish.

Eliza's head rested against Marco's chest, his arms wrapped protectively around her. The quiet of the island night settled around them like a soft blanket, the distant call of a nocturnal creature punctuating the silence. They remained entwined, not speaking, their bodies communicating everything that needed to be said.

As the bioluminescence waned and the moon climbed higher in the sky, the moment held them suspended in time, a perfect capsule of beauty and intimacy amidst the chaos of their survival. In this place, with this man, Eliza had found not just a sanctuary from the storm, but a sanctuary within herself—a sanctuary that promised to hold them both, no matter what was yet to come.

———◆◇◆———

Dawn's first light crept across the beach, painting the sand in soft pastels. Eliza lay on her side, head propped on her elbow, watching Marco's chest rise and fall with each peaceful breath. His features, usually sharp with concentration, had softened in sleep. A lock of dark hair fell across his forehead, and her fingers itched to brush it away, to feel the warmth of his skin once more.

The memory of their night in the lagoon sent warmth flooding through her body, a delicious shiver that started at her spine and radiated outward. She traced the curve of his shoulder with her eyes, remembering how his skin had felt beneath her fingertips, how the bioluminescent water had transformed them both into creatures of light and shadow, magical and otherworldly in their shared moment of connection.

But in the harsh reality of morning, doubt gnawed at the edges of her contentment, persistent as the tide itself. What would people think? What would her family say? She'd been the wife of a wealthy man for so long, groomed for a life of luxury and social expectations, each day mapped out in careful increments of appropriate behavior. Now here she was, falling for a man who worked with his hands, who knew the sea like she knew designer labels, whose calluses told stories of real work and authentic living.

Marco shifted in his sleep, his arm reaching out as if searching for her, fingers curling slightly in the empty air. Her heart clenched at the gesture, so unguarded and genuine. This wasn't just attraction or the heightened emotions of survival. This was deeper, more real than anything she'd experienced in her carefully curated life before the shipwreck, a connection that seemed to bypass all her learned defenses.

She thought of Richard, still sleeping in his separate shelter, clinging to the remnants of their old social hierarchy like a life preserver. How different he seemed now, his polished façade crumbling under the pressure of real adversity, revealing the hollow space where substance should have been. While Marco ... Marco had shown her strength she never knew she possessed, taught her to find beauty in struggle, helped her discover the woman beneath years of social conditioning.

Sand crunched beneath her feet as she sat up, wrapping her arms around her knees. The rising sun cast long shadows across the beach, and she watched them stretch and transform, much like her own perceptions had since washing up on these shores. Everything she'd once thought important - the galas, the social climbing, the endless pursuit of status - seemed trivial now, replaced by simpler, more vital truths: survival, companionship, the raw honesty of feelings unfettered by social constraints. The island had stripped away her pretenses, layer by careful layer, until only her essence remained.

Yet still that voice whispered, persistent as the waves lapping at the shore: What happens if they're rescued? Could what they'd found here survive in the real world, or would it dissolve like salt in water, leaving behind only the ache of what might have been?

Marco's eyes fluttered open, squinting against the harsh morning light that filtered through the palm fronds above. His hand found Eliza's, fingers intertwining naturally, seeking that familiar comfort they'd come to depend on.

"Morning." He pushed himself up, sand cascading from his shoulders in tiny rivulets. "We need to check the fish traps. And that water collection system needs reinforcing before the next storm hits. The last one nearly took out the whole structure."

"The palm fronds we used are already starting to decay. The salt air's eating through them faster than we expected." Eliza picked up a fallen coconut, examining its husk with the practiced eye she'd developed over their time here. "But look - we could use these fibers instead. They're stronger, more durable. Nature's own rope, just waiting to be used."

Marco ran his thumb across the rough surface, feeling each fibrous strand. "Smart thinking. Though it'll take twice as long to process them. We'll need to soak them properly, strip them down."

"Time we have. Resources we don't." She gestured at their makeshift camp, where every scrap and fragment had been carefully repurposed. "Each problem we face is teaching us something new. Like these coconuts - they're not just food and water. They're tools, materials. Everything here has multiple uses, if we're clever enough to see them."

"You make it sound so simple." His shoulders tensed, betraying the weight of responsibility he carried. "But one mistake, one miscalculation out here, and we could lose everything we've built."

Eliza squeezed his hand, her grip firm and reassuring. "That's why we work together. You know the sea, the weather patterns better than anyone. I'm learning to see possibilities in everything around us. Between the two of us, we've got this. We're stronger as a team."

"Never thought I'd hear such optimism from someone who used to complain about hotel room bedroom sheet thread counts." A smile tugged at his lips, warming his weathered features. "The woman who brought three suitcases of designer clothes for a week-long cruise."

"Maybe I needed to lose everything to find what really matters." She leaned against him, drawing strength from his solid presence. "Every challenge is an opportunity to grow stronger, smarter. Like that reef barrier - it's not just an obstacle. It's protecting us from the worst waves, creating a safe zone for fishing. We just had to learn to work with it instead of fighting against it."

Marco's expression softened as he studied her face, seeing the strength that had emerged from her former fragility. "You've come so far from that first day on the raft. When you couldn't even look at the water without trembling."

"We both have. And we'll keep adapting, keep solving each problem as it comes. That's what survival is - endless adaptation." She stood, brushing sand from her legs with calloused hands that no longer flinched at manual labor. "Now, about those fish traps - I have an idea for improving the design. Something I noticed about the tidal patterns yesterday."

Chapter Sixteen

The Signal

A glint of metal caught Eliza's eye as she waded through the shallows, checking the fish traps. At first, she dismissed it as sunlight dancing on the waves, but something about its steady presence made her pause. Her heart skipped when she spotted it again - distinct and unmistakable against the horizon.

"Marco!" Her voice cracked as she scrambled onto the beach. "Marco, come quick!"

He emerged from the tree line, arms full of palm fronds. "What's wrong?"

"Look!" She pointed toward the horizon, where a dark shape broke the endless blue. "Out there - I think it's a ship!"

The fronds scattered at his feet as he shielded his eyes, scanning the distance. His whole body tensed. "Container vessel. Heading northwest."

Richard burst from his shelter, hair wild from sleep. "A ship? Where?"

"We need the signal fire." Marco sprinted to their prepared pile of green leaves and damp wood. "Eliza, the matches from the emergency kit. Richard, help me with this tarp."

Eliza's hands trembled as she dug through their supplies. The waterproof case felt slick in her grip. Her chest tightened - their first sign of civilization in weeks. Her fingers fumbled with the matches, dropping two before striking one successfully.

The leaves caught quickly, sending thick white smoke into the cloudless sky. Marco and Richard stretched the orange tarp between them, waving it high.

"They have to see us." Richard's voice hitched. "They have to."

Eliza stared at the vessel, willing it to turn. The smoke column grew, rising straight up in the still air. Perfect conditions. Perfect visibility. Her throat closed around unspoken prayers as she watched the ship continue its steady course.

"Come on," Marco muttered, his muscles straining as he held the tarp higher. "Look this way. Just look this way."

The minutes stretched like hours as they watched, hoped, prayed. The ship maintained its heading, neither slowing nor changing course. Its hull gleamed in the morning sun, tantalizingly close yet impossibly far.

As the ship continued its course, an unexpected weight settled in Eliza's chest. Her arms lowered, the urgency of their signals fading. The life she'd left behind - a perfect appearance, charity galas, endless social obligations - felt distant, dreamlike.

Marco stepped closer, his voice low. "Something's wrong?"

"I just..." She gestured at their makeshift camp, the crystal waters, the untamed beauty surrounding them. "We've built something here. Something real."

His calloused hand found hers, rough against smooth. "We could stay. Build more than just shelters. Make this place our own."

"You'd want that?"

"Been thinking about it. I know, it's an insane thought. No deadlines, no pressure. Just us, living by our own rules." His thumb traced circles on her palm. "There'll be other ships."

The freedom of choice hit her like a wave. Every morning, she'd woken to purpose - fishing, foraging, creating. No phones ringing, no expectations crushing her spirit. Here, she was just Eliza, not the perfect arm piece for her husband.

Richard's voice cut through her thoughts. "It's turning! The ship - look!"

But it wasn't. The vessel grew smaller, its wake a white ribbon stretching toward the horizon. Eliza watched it go, her breath steady, her heart light.

"We lost it." Richard slumped to the sand. "Our chance..."

Marco squeezed her hand. "You okay?"

She turned to him, seeing the same peace in his eyes that she felt in her soul. The ship might have carried them back to civilization, but it would have taken something precious in return. Here, among the palms and endless stars, she'd found a different kind of wealth.

"More than okay." She smiled, watching the smoke dissipate into the clear blue sky. "I think I finally understand what being rescued really means."

Richard kicked the smoldering remains of their signal fire, sending embers scattering across the sand. "You did this on purpose. Both of you!"

"What are you talking about?" Marco stepped between Richard and the fire.

"I saw you two." Richard jabbed a finger at Eliza. "Holding hands, whispering. You didn't want that ship to see us."

Eliza's face flushed. "That's ridiculous. We all worked to signal-"

"Worked?" Richard's laugh cut sharp as broken glass. "You dropped half the matches. And you-" He turned on Marco. "Taking your sweet time with that tarp. I was the only one actually trying to get us rescued!"

Marco's jaw tightened. "Watch yourself, Richard."

"Or what? You'll strand us here forever? Play survivor man with my wife?"

"Your wife?" Eliza stepped forward, her voice steady. "I haven't been your wife since the moment this island showed me who you really are."

Richard's face twisted. "What's that supposed to mean?"

"While we built shelters, found food, kept us alive - what did you do? Complain. Sleep. Demand we serve you like some island resort."

"I was sick!"

"You were weak." The words fell from her lips like stones. "And now you're just pathetic."

Richard lunged toward her. Marco caught his arm, spinning him away with practiced ease. Richard stumbled, landing hard in the sand.

"Don't." Marco's voice carried the weight of weeks of built trust and respect. "Just don't."

Richard pushed himself up, sand clinging to his designer clothes - now ragged and salt-stained. His eyes darted between them, seeing for the first time how they stood together, unified. The power he'd wielded in their old world meant nothing here.

"Fine." He backed away. "Fine. You two deserve each other. Deserve this whole damn island."

Eliza watched him retreat toward his shelter, shoulders hunched. The man she'd married disappeared with each step, replaced by a stranger she'd never truly known.

Marco touched her elbow. "You okay?"

She nodded, surprised to find she meant it. "Better than okay. Free."

The moon cast silver ribbons across the lagoon as Eliza walked along the shore. Her bare feet left temporary impressions in the wet sand, each step washing away with the gentle tide. The night breeze carried the sweet scent of tropical flowers mingled with salt spray. She found Marco sitting on their favorite driftwood log, staring out at the endless horizon where the ship had disappeared hours ago.

He shifted, making space for her, the weathered wood creaking beneath his movement. "Couldn't sleep either?"

"Too many thoughts." She settled beside him, close enough to feel his warmth. The rough bark pressed familiar patterns into her skin.

"About the ship?"

"About everything. This island. Us." She traced patterns in the sand with her toes, watching tiny crabs scuttle away from her movements. "How different everything feels now."

Marco turned to face her, his features softened by moonlight. The gentle breeze ruffled his dark hair. "I've never felt more alive than these past weeks. With you."

"Marco-"

"Let me finish." His hand found hers, rough calluses against soft skin. His fingers trembled slightly, betraying his nervousness. "I know what I am. A crew member. Someone who'd never get a second glance at those fancy parties you used to attend. But here? Here I'm just a man who's fallen in love with an amazing woman."

Her breath caught. The confession hung between them, heavy with possibility. Palm fronds rustled overhead, nature's whispered accompaniment to this moment.

"What you had with Richard - that wasn't real. It was a business deal dressed up as marriage. But this?" He gestured to their surroundings, to the pristine beach stretching endlessly in both directions. "This is pure. Honest."

"Everything's simpler here," she whispered, letting her fingers intertwine with his. The calluses on his palm told stories of hard work and survival.

"Money doesn't matter on this beach. Status doesn't matter in that shelter we built together." His free hand brushed her cheek, thumb grazing the slight sunburn there. "Tell me you feel it too."

Eliza leaned into his touch, her heart racing. The pulse in her throat fluttered like trapped butterflies. "I feel... everything. You've shown me what it means to truly live, Marco. To be valued for who I am, not what I represent."

She left the declaration hanging, neither confirming nor denying the depth of her feelings. The waves lapped at the shore in steady rhythm, marking time in this suspended moment. Her response seemed to satisfy him as he pulled her closer, pressing his lips to her forehead.

"We'll figure it out," he murmured against her skin. "Together."

CHAPTER SEVENTEEN

Distant Horizons

Marco wiped sweat from his brow as he arranged freshly picked flowers on the makeshift bamboo table. Six months had transformed their camp into a proper settlement - thatched-roof huts replaced temporary shelters, a garden flourished with island produce, and even Richard had found his place maintaining their fish traps.

"Need any help?" Richard approached, carrying a string of fresh fish. The hostility between them had faded into grudging respect.

"Just finishing up. Thanks for getting dinner." Marco tucked a vibrant red bloom into the center of his arrangement.

"Hard to believe it's been half a year." Richard cleaned the fish with practiced movements. "Remember how useless I was that first week?"

"You've come a long way." Marco grinned. "We all have."

Their camp had evolved into an efficient system. Marco's knowledge merged with Eliza's organizational skills and Richard's unexpected talent for crafting tools. They'd learned to smoke fish, preserve fruit, and even brew a passable coconut wine.

"Eliza still out gathering?"

"Yeah, I sent her to the far beach. Wanted time to set this up." Marco gestured to his surprise - a feast laid out on broad leaves, decorated with shells and flowers. "Six months since we landed here. Thought we should celebrate how far we've come."

Richard nodded, understanding in his eyes. The island had stripped away their old roles, rebuilt them into stronger versions of themselves. Eliza had blossomed from society wife to confident survivor. Marco's quiet competence had earned him natural leadership. Even Richard had shed his corporate armor to find purpose in simple work.

"She'll love it." Richard carried the cleaned fish to their smoking rack. "I'll make myself scarce tonight."

Marco added final touches to the celebration space - torches for when darkness fell, cushions woven from palm fronds, that bottle of coconut wine they'd been saving. He'd even carved her a gift - a delicate hair comb decorated with tiny shells.

The sound of footsteps approaching made him straighten. Eliza appeared through the trees, her basket full of fruit, hair sun-streaked and skin glowing with health. She stopped short at the sight of the decorated clearing.

"Marco?" Her eyes widened as she took in the scene. "What's all this?"

Eliza set her basket down, fingers trailing over the flower arrangements. "I never thought I'd say this, but I'm grateful for what happened. For ending up here." She settled onto a palm cushion, her movements fluid and natural. "Back home, I was just playing a part. Here, I'm actually living."

Marco joined her, pouring the coconut wine into shells. "You've changed. We all have."

"Remember my meltdown over broken nails that first week?" She laughed, examining her strong, capable hands. "Now I can build a fire, weave baskets, catch fish with my bare hands."

"What happens when we're rescued?" Marco's voice was soft.

"I don't want to go back to that empty life." Eliza leaned against him. "We could build something real. Maybe somewhere remote, where we can use what we've learned. A place of our own."

"A beach house? Small farm?"

"With a garden like this one. And we'll teach others what we know." Her eyes sparkled. "No more charity galas. Just honest work and simple pleasures."

From the tree line, Richard watched the couple's intimate conversation. His fingers traced the edge of his journal where he'd documented every detail of their survival. The skills, the innovations, the transformation. Knowledge worth a fortune to the right publisher. His eyes calculated the potential - survival memoirs, self-help books, speaking tours.

Eliza's laughter drifted across the clearing. She looked nothing like the polished socialite who'd boarded the Aurora. Her movements matched the island's rhythm - confident, purposeful, free. The setting sun painted her skin golden as she showed Marco a new weaving pattern she'd discovered.

"The moon will be full tonight." She gestured to the darkening sky. "Perfect for a night swim."

"You've gotten better at reading weather patterns than me."

"This is home now." Eliza's voice held certainty. "Even if rescue came tomorrow, part of me would miss this place. The simplicity. The truth of it."

Marco presented the carved comb. Eliza ran her fingers over the intricate shell work, her expression soft with appreciation for craftsmanship that would have seemed primitive to her former self.

CHAPTER EIGHTEEN

Rescue Signs

Dawn painted the sky in gentle strokes of pink and gold. Eliza traced patterns on Marco's chest, their bodies nestled in the softness of woven palm fronds beneath their shelter.

"The waves sound different at sunrise." She pressed her ear against his skin, listening to his heartbeat mix with the distant surf.

"That's because the wind shifts with the warming air." Marco's fingers wandered through her hair, catching on small tangles. "The whole island wakes up differently."

"I used to need three cups of coffee before I could form a sentence this early." Eliza propped herself up on an elbow, studying his face in the growing light. "Now I can't imagine sleeping past dawn."

"Miss your espresso machine?"

"Not as much as I thought I would." She touched the rough stubble on his jaw.

Marco caught her hand, kissed her palm. "Remember how you used to flinch when my hands were calloused?"

"Now I love how they feel." Eliza shifted closer, skin warm against his. "Everything's different. The way you smell like salt and wood smoke. How the sun feels on my back. Even the air tastes better here."

A gentle breeze carried the scent of morning flowers through their shelter. Marco wrapped a strand of her hair around his finger, watching it catch the light.

"You're different too." His voice was soft. "The way you move, how you carry yourself. Like you finally fit in your own skin."

"Because I'm not pretending anymore." Eliza rested her chin on his chest. "No more perfect makeup or designer clothes. Just me."

"Just you is pretty perfect."

She smiled, tracing the scar on his shoulder. "We should get up. Check the fish traps before the tide changes."

"Five more minutes." Marco pulled her closer. "The fish can wait."

The distant drone of engines cut through their conversation. Marco's head snapped up, scanning the sky. A glint of metal caught the morning sun.

"The signal fire - now!" Marco sprinted to their prepared pile of green palm fronds.

Eliza grabbed the coconut-shell torch they'd kept ready for months. Her hands shook as she struck the flint. The spark caught, and thick white smoke billowed skyward.

Richard emerged from his shelter, waving a reflective panel salvaged from their raft. The plane banked, circling lower.

"They've seen us." Marco's voice cracked. He grabbed Eliza's hand, squeezing tight.

The aircraft waggled its wings in acknowledgment, dropping a small package that landed on the beach. Inside they found a radio and instructions - rescue would arrive within 24 hours.

Eliza stared at the paper, her throat tight. "It doesn't feel real."

"Having second thoughts?" Marco pulled her close.

"About rescue? No. About going back to that life? Absolutely."

Richard paced the beach, muttering about book deals and interviews. The old ambition had crept back into his voice.

"I meant what I said last night." Eliza traced patterns in the sand. "I want that little beach house. A garden. Simple work."

Marco nodded. "I know a place in Costa Rica. Tiny fishing village. Could use someone with boat repair skills."

"And someone who knows how to weave palm fronds into actual furniture?" Eliza smiled.

"The locals would love you. We could build something there, teach survival skills to rich tourists looking for thrills and adventure."

"No more charity boards or corporate parties?"

"Just sunsets and fresh fish and making things with our hands."

They sat in comfortable silence, watching waves crash on their beach. Tomorrow would bring helicopters, reporters, a return to civilization. But they'd carry this place within them - its lessons, its clarity, its truth.

"Promise me something?" Eliza pressed her shoulder against his. "Promise we won't let them turn this into some glossy survival story. What happened here was real. Sacred almost."

"I promise." Marco pulled out the shell comb he'd carved, sliding it into her hair. "We'll build our own paradise. One palm frond at a time."

Richard watched Marco and Eliza from the shade of a palm tree, his jaw tight. The casual intimacy between them twisted his features into a mask of calculation. His once manicured fingers drummed against his thigh as he studied their easy laughter, their shared glances, his silver signet ring catching the tropical sun with each agitated tap.

He straightened his salt-stained shirt and strode toward them, designer loafers sinking awkwardly in the sand. "Eliza, darling. A moment?"

She looked up, her hand still intertwined with Marco's, sun-bleached hair falling loose around her shoulders.

"Think about what's waiting back home. The penthouse view of Central Park, my mother's charity galas." Richard's voice dripped honey, each word precisely chosen. "The life we built. Your closet full of Louboutins. Remember how stunning you looked at the Met Gala? How everyone whispered about us being the perfect power couple?"

Eliza's bare feet dug into the warm sand. She glanced down at her calloused hands, strong from months of weaving shelters and gathering food, remembering how they once trembled holding champagne flutes at cocktail parties. "That life feels hollow now, Richard. Like a beautiful empty shell."

"You can't be serious. Trading everything for... what? Playing Robinson Crusoe with the help? Have you lost your mind in this heat?"

"He was never 'the help.' That's exactly what I'm leaving behind - that entitled mindset." She stood, shoulders straight, ocean breeze lifting her hair. "I know who I am now. What I want. No more pretending."

The woman who stepped off the Aurora months ago would have flinched at Richard's sneer, would have wavered at the mention of designer shoes and social status. But that woman had washed away in the storm, replaced by someone who understood the difference between surviving and truly living.

"I've never been more certain of anything." Eliza's voice rang clear and strong across the beach. "I choose this path. The simple life, honest work, real connection. You can keep your galas and empty conversations."

Marco remained silent, letting her stand in her own power. His weathered hands remained steady in his lap as he watched her face her past. She'd earned this moment, this declaration of independence.

The transformation was complete. The society debutante who once fretted over place settings now read weather patterns in the clouds. The woman who had delegated every task to others could build a shelter with her own hands. Most importantly, she'd found her voice - and she was using it to write her own story, one that had nothing to do with society columns or expectations.

CHAPTER NINETEEN

Last Island Night

The sunset painted the beach in amber and rose, their last evening before civilization would reclaim them. Even Richard had shed his usual complaints, stretched out on a handwoven mat near their signal fire, his calloused hands folded behind his head.

"Remember that first coconut we tried to crack?" Eliza passed around fresh mango slices, the juice glistening on her fingers like amber drops. "We spent hours just staring at it, wondering where to begin."

"Went flying straight into the ocean." Marco's laugh rumbled deep in his chest, echoing across the beach. "Good thing we got better at it. Those first few weeks were rough."

Richard raised his portion of fruit, the firelight catching the new scars on his hands. "To survival skills we never knew we had. And to never taking room service for granted again."

The simple gesture sparked something rare between them - a shared acknowledgment of their journey. The fire crackled, sending sparks dancing into the darkening sky, each ember a memory of their time here.

"The stars." Eliza leaned back on her elbows, her sun-bleached hair falling loose around her shoulders. "I'll miss seeing them like this, so clear and close. The city lights could never compare to this."

Marco traced the constellations with his finger, his movements sure and practiced after countless nights of stargazing. "Southern Cross. Led ancient sailors home. Guided us through some dark nights too."

"Home." The word hung between them, heavy with meaning. Each knew tomorrow would redefine that concept entirely, their old lives waiting like distant dreams.

As night deepened, they drifted apart for private moments with their island sanctuary. Richard walked the shoreline, his silhouette straight and purposeful, perhaps already rehearsing his return to boardrooms and business deals, though his steps faltered near their old fishing spot.

Eliza climbed to their freshwater pool, trailing her fingers through the cool water that had sustained them for so long. The jungle sounds wrapped around her like a familiar embrace - birds calling their evening songs, leaves rustling in the breeze, the distant crash of waves. She'd found herself here, stripped of pretense and polish, transformed by necessity and nature.

Marco stood at the surf's edge, waves lapping at his feet, the salt spray familiar as his own breath now. He picked up a piece of driftwood, smoothed by salt and time, and ran his hands along its weathered surface. The island had revealed their true natures - his strength in leading them through crisis, Eliza's resilience in the face of despair, Richard's surprising adaptability when stripped of power and privilege.

The air grew thick with unspoken goodbyes, with the sweet ache of ending something profound. Paradise had changed them in ways rescue couldn't undo. Their bare feet in warm sand, the taste of wild fruit on their tongues, the rhythm of days measured by sun and tide - these moments had carved new paths in their hearts, creating bonds that would outlast their exile.

The distant thrum grew louder, cutting through the morning mist. Marco dropped the coconut he'd been collecting, his eyes fixed on the horizon. The sound pulled them like magnets to the beach's center, their hearts pounding with a mixture of hope and trepidation.

"There!" Eliza pointed at a dark speck that emerged from the clouds, her finger trembling slightly.

The helicopter's rotors whipped the sand into stinging clouds, forcing them to shield their faces. Palm fronds bent and swayed as the aircraft descended, its sleek metal body reflecting the morning sun like a mirage, a mechanical intruder in their primitive sanctuary.

Richard stumbled backward, his calloused feet digging into the sand. "It's real. It's actually real."

The door slid open, revealing figures in crisp blue uniforms. Their boots hit the sand with military precision, radios crackling with static and voices. The rescuers' clean-shaven faces and pressed clothes seemed alien against the wild backdrop of their beach, like visitors from another world entirely.

"I'm Lieutenant Cooper, US Coast Guard." A tall woman approached, her clipboard and pen incongruous artifacts of civilization. Her precise movements and authoritative stance belonged to a reality they'd almost forgotten. "Are you the survivors from the Aurora?"

Eliza touched her tangled hair, suddenly aware of her sun-roughened skin and makeshift clothing. The lieutenant's perfume - subtle and artificial - made her head spin with memories of department stores and office buildings.

"Yes, we..." Marco's voice cracked. He cleared his throat, struggling to match the formal tone, to bridge the gap between their world and the one that had just landed on their shore. "Three survivors. We lost Captain Reynolds and two crew members in the storm."

A medic approached with a modern first-aid kit, its pristine white plastic jarring against their wooden spears and woven baskets. Richard flinched when the man touched his arm to check his vitals, his body unused to the clinical contact.

"Mr. Harrington?" Another rescuer consulted a tablet, its screen glowing unnaturally in the morning light. "Your company's been searching for months. There's a board meeting scheduled-"

"Board meeting?" Richard barked out a laugh, gesturing at their shelter, at the life they'd built from nothing. "I haven't even worn shoes in months."

The lieutenant's radio crackled. "Base, we've located all three. Preparing for extraction."

Eliza watched the rescuers move through their camp, taking photos, marking coordinates. Their efficiency felt like an invasion, reducing their survival to data points and rescue protocols. The plastic tags they attached to their belongings seemed to strip away months of meaning with each clinical label. She caught Marco's eye across the chaos, recognizing in his stance the same disorientation she felt - their wild freedom already beginning to recede like the morning tide, replaced by the encroaching weight of civilization.

CHAPTER TWENTY

Return to Society

C amera flashes exploded like lightning across the hospital lobby, casting harsh shadows that danced across the institutional tile floors. Microphones thrust forward like spears, reporters shouting questions that blurred into white noise, their voices echoing off the sterile walls. Eliza pressed herself against the wall, the antiseptic hospital scent mixing with expensive cologne from the media crowd, making her head swim.

"Mr. Harrington, how did you survive? What did you eat?"

"Over here! Ms. Harrington, what was it like being stranded? Did you ever lose hope?"

Richard stepped forward, his hospital gown replaced with a charcoal pinstripe suit that seemed to materialize within hours of their rescue, complete with a silk pocket square and gleaming oxfords. His unshaven face and wild hair had vanished, replaced by careful grooming that made their island experience seem like a distant dream, as if the salt air and desperation had never touched him.

"The human spirit is remarkably resilient." Richard's voice carried across the lobby with practiced ease, the same tone he used for shareholder meetings. "This experience has given me unique insights into crisis management and leadership under pressure - lessons I'll be implementing at Harrington Global to drive innovation and growth."

Eliza's stomach turned, bile rising in her throat. Six months of watching him huddle in their shelter, complaining about coconuts and refusing to help with fishing, whining about the heat and insects, yet here he stood spinning their survival into corporate gold, as if he'd been some kind of island CEO.

"My upcoming book 'Surviving Success' will detail how island survival mirrors the business world, offering unique perspectives on resource management and team dynamics." Richard flashed his camera-ready smile, teeth gleaming under the fluorescent lights. "My team's already fielding calls from multiple publishers, and we're exploring media rights."

Marco pushed through the crowd, his borrowed clothes hanging loose on his frame, the hospital-issued shirt several sizes too big. A reporter shoved a microphone in his face, nearly catching his chin. "Sources say you were the yacht's mechanic. How does it feel knowing you kept a Millionaire alive? Will you be returning to your job?"

Security guards formed a barrier between the press and the survivors, their dark suits creating a wall of authority, but cameras clicked through the gaps like persistent insects. Headlines already screamed across phones and tablets: "CEO's Island Ordeal", "180 Days Lost at Sea", "Harrington's Return Shakes Markets", "Paradise Lost: A CEO's Journey".

"Harrington Global stock jumped twelve points on news of your rescue," a business reporter called out, her sharp blazer a slash of red in the crowd. "Any comment on the market response?"

Richard straightened his tie, smoothing it with manicured fingers that showed no trace of the calluses they'd developed. "I've scheduled a shareholders' meeting for tomorrow. Our Q3 projections-"

Eliza turned away, the fluorescent lights suddenly too harsh, too artificial. Their island world of simple survival - the daily rhythm of waves, the struggle for food, the honest sweat of existence - felt more real than this circus of cameras and corporate spin. Through the glass doors, she glimpsed more reporters arriving, satellite trucks lining the street, their antennae reaching toward the sky like metal palm trees, broadcasting their story to a world that seemed increasingly foreign.

Marco pressed his back against the cool hospital wall, hands stuffed in the pockets of his borrowed khakis. A camera flash caught his face, and he blinked away the afterimage, remembering the stark island sunlight that had guided them to fresh water and food. This artificial lightning felt wrong, invasive.

"Just a few questions, Marco," a reporter pressed. "Your background in mechanics-"

"I did what anyone would do." Marco's voice stayed quiet, steady. His gaze drifted to the window, where palm trees swayed in the parking lot. Different trees than their island, manicured and tame, but still a comfort.

Eliza stepped between microphones, her practiced smile a shield. "We're grateful for everyone's interest, but we need time to process our experience." Her designer clothes, rushed to the hospital by her assistant, felt stiff after months of salt-weathered fabric. "Marco's skills and knowledge were invaluable. We wouldn't be here without him."

Richard materialized at her elbow, his Patek Philippe watch catching the light. "Darling, the Governor's office called. They're sending a car." He touched her arm, his fingers lingering. "And the jet's fueled up whenever you're ready to head back to the estate. No need for commercial flights."

"I thought we agreed to give statements to the press first." Eliza shifted away from his touch.

"Of course, of course." Richard's laugh echoed across marble floors. "Though the Four Seasons has already prepared the presidential suite. Much more comfortable than these...institutio nal surroundings." His eyes flicked to Marco, then back to Eliza. "We should discuss the foundation's new survival education initiative over dinner. Just the two of us."

Marco pushed off from the wall, his movements deliberate and contained. A security guard appeared at his side, ready to clear a path through the press. Their eyes met across the lobby - Marco's steady gaze finding Eliza's - before the crowd surged between them like a tide.

Marco sat on the edge of the hospital bed, his worn duffel bag packed with the few belongings he'd accumulated since their rescue. The fluorescent lights cast a sterile glow across the linoleum floor, so different from the warm island sunlight that had witnessed his growing connection with Eliza.

He checked his watch - the simple digital one the hospital had provided, nothing like Richard's flashy timepiece. 2:55 PM. Five minutes until Eliza would arrive, just as they'd planned during their whispered conversation in the hospital garden, away from the circus of reporters and Richard's calculating gaze.

The small bag contained everything he owned: two changes of clothes from the hospital donation bin, a paperback left by a nurse, and a piece of coral he'd kept from the beach where they'd first washed ashore. Where Eliza had first looked at him not as a member of the yacht's crew, but as the man who kept them alive.

His fingers traced the coral's rough surface through the canvas of his bag. Six months on the island had stripped away their social barriers, revealed their true selves. While Richard schemed about book deals and movie rights, Eliza had seen through the artifice of their old lives.

"Ready for a real adventure?" She'd whispered yesterday, her eyes bright with possibility. "No cameras, no press conferences, no corporate spin."

The wall clock ticked past 2:57. Marco stood, shouldering his bag. Their plan was simple - skip the press circus downstairs, take the service elevator to the parking garage where Eliza would meet him with her car. Head west, away from Richard's carefully orchestrated media narrative and the suffocating expectations of their old lives.

He moved to the window, watching the parking garage entrance. A few minutes more and they'd be gone, leaving behind the artificial world of press conferences and corporate maneuvering. On the island, they'd discovered what mattered - survival, trust, the simple truth of two people facing life's challenges together.

The clock hit 3:00 PM. Marco smiled, picking up his bag. Time to begin their new chapter.

The door clicked open. Marco turned, smile fading as Eliza stepped in wearing a cream Chanel suit, pearls gleaming at her throat. Through the open door, Richard leaned against the corridor wall, examining his phone with casual possession, his tailored Italian suit a stark reminder of the world they'd left behind.

"The car's waiting downstairs." Eliza's voice carried the crisp tone of quarterly reports and charity galas, devoid of the warmth it had held during their island nights. "I came to say goodbye."

Marco's bag slipped from numb fingers, hitting the carpet with a soft thud. "Goodbye? We had plans. The survival school for the wealthy, starting fresh- everything we talked about under the stars."

"That was island talk." She smoothed invisible wrinkles from her skirt, her perfectly manicured nails catching the fluorescent light. "Reality's different here. You must understand that."

"Reality? We built shelters together, found food, survived-" His voice cracked, memories of rain-soaked nights and shared victories flooding back. "You said you loved me."

"I needed you there. You kept us alive." Her manicured fingers tapped her designer purse, a nervous tell he'd noticed during their first week together. "But I need what Richard provides now. The foundation, the lifestyle, my position on the board. The connections that took years to build."

Marco stepped forward, reaching for her hand, remembering how those same fingers had once woven palm fronds for their shelter. "The connection we had was real. You said yourself Richard was weak, useless- you saw through all this."

"Survival skills and business acumen are different things." Her eyes, once warm with firelight and shared dreams, now held the cold calculation of profit margins and shareholder meetings. "Richard understands my world. The social obligations, the expectations. The nuances you never quite grasped."

"Your world?" Marco's chest tightened as six months of memories - shared laughter, stolen kisses under palm trees, whispered plans for their future - crumbled like sand castles at high tide. "Everything you said about starting over, about finding what matters- about building something real-"

"What matters is maintaining my lifestyle." Her smile held the same practiced charm she'd shown the reporters, perfectly rehearsed and utterly empty. "The island was temporary. This is permanent. These are the choices that define us."

Marco stared at this stranger in designer clothes, searching for traces of the woman who'd helped him spear fish, who'd cried in his arms during storms, who'd sworn the corporate world was a hollow façade. The mask had dropped completely, revealing a creature of boardrooms and balance sheets, of calculated moves and measured returns.

"You never meant any of it." The truth hit like a physical blow, shattering his carefully constructed future.

"Business is business." She turned toward the door, her heels clicking against the floor like a gavel falling. "Richard's waiting."

Marco's legs gave out and he slumped against the hospital bed, his chest heaving with silent sobs. The coral fragment fell from his bag, skittering across the linoleum floor like his shattered dreams. His calloused fingers pressed against his eyes, but couldn't stop the tears that burned down his cheeks, each drop a bitter reminder of his naivety.

The scent of her designer perfume still lingered in the sterile air - so different from the salt and sweat that had marked their island days. He remembered her laugh when they'd caught their first fish together, the way her eyes lit up when he taught her to make rope from palm fibers, the softness of her touch during those long nights when the stars seemed close enough to touch. The memories felt like daggers now, twisting deeper with each breath.

"God, I'm such a fool." His voice cracked, echoing in the empty room. Every shared moment, every whispered promise, every plan they'd made - all calculated moves in her survival game. While he'd been falling in love with her true self, she'd been playing a role, using his skills to stay alive until rescue arrived. The realization made him sick to his stomach, bile rising in his throat.

His hands shook as he picked up the coral piece, its rough edges cutting into his palm. The pain felt distant compared to the hollow ache in his chest. On the island, stripped of society's pretenses, he'd believed they'd found something real. Something pure. But for her, it had just been another business transaction - survival skills exchanged for temporary affection, as coldly calculated as any merger deal.

The click of her heels faded down the corridor, taking with her the future he'd imagined. Building their survival school together, sharing their knowledge, making a life that meant something. All gone, replaced by the harsh reality that he'd been nothing more than a convenient tool in her journey back to wealth and power. The dreams they'd shared now seemed as fragile as morning mist.

Tears dripped onto his borrowed clothes as memories flooded back - her head on his shoulder during storm-tossed nights, her fingers intertwined with his as they watched sunsets, her voice soft and sincere as she'd promised they'd build something real together once they were rescued. Each memory now tainted, poisoned by the knowledge that every moment had been a calculated performance, every tender touch a lie crafted for survival. The weight of truth crushed against his chest, leaving him gasping in the sterile hospital air.

CHAPTER TWENTY-ONE

Return to the Golden Cage

The elevator doors parted to reveal the sprawling Manhattan penthouse. Richard stepped out first, arms spread wide like a returning king. Marble floors gleamed beneath crystal chandeliers, floor-to-ceiling windows framing the city skyline like a living painting. The scent of fresh orchids - his secretary must have arranged for fresh flowers - mingled with the familiar notes of leather and wealth.

"Home sweet home." Richard made a beeline for the wet bar, ice cubes clinking against crystal. "God, I missed civilization." He poured three fingers of his favorite single malt, the amber liquid catching the light.

Eliza trailed behind, her designer heels echoing through the vast space. Camera flashes from the street below still sparkled in her vision - dozens of reporters clamoring for shots of the devoted wife supporting her recovered husband. Their shouted questions still rang in her ears: "Mrs. Harrington , how does it feel to be home?"

"Such an inspiring story of loyalty," the Today Show host had gushed that morning, while Eliza smiled her camera-ready smile, perfectly practiced during countless society events. "Standing by your husband through such an ordeal."

"In sickness and in health." The words had tasted like ash on her tongue. "That's what marriage means." She'd clutched her designer handbag tighter, knuckles white beneath her manicure.

The media ate it up - the perfect wife, the perfect ending. Photos of her helping Richard at press conferences splashed across every magazine, each one carefully staged for maximum impact. "Love Conquers All" the headlines declared, while Richard worked the sympathy angle, describing his "brave battle with seasickness" during their ordeal. No mention of the truth, of course. That wouldn't fit the narrative.

Now, alone in her marble bathroom, Eliza stared at her reflection. Designer dress, perfect makeup, not a hair out of place. Everything exactly as it should be. Her fingers traced the smooth countertop, so different from rough-hewn bamboo. The scent of expensive perfume replaced memories of salt air and campfire smoke. She could almost feel the phantom warmth of those flames on her skin.

She moved through the penthouse like a ghost, past the art pieces worth more than most people made in a year - a Picasso here, a Monet there, each one selected to impress. Richard's voice drifted from his study, already back to making deals, barking orders into his phone as if he'd never left. The city sparkled beyond the windows, a sea of lights replacing the star-filled sky she'd grown to love, the constellations she'd learned to map with different eyes.

Her hand brushed the silk sheets of their king-sized bed. So soft. So comfortable. So empty. She sank onto the edge, surrounded by every luxury she'd fought to keep. Her carefully maintained smile slipped, just for a moment, in the privacy of her gilded cage. In the distance, a helicopter's searchlight swept across the sky, and her heart skipped a beat, remembering a different kind of escape.

A commotion erupted in the lobby below. Eliza crossed to the window, drawn by raised voices and the crackle of security radios.

"Sir, you need to leave the premises." The doorman's voice carried through the intercom.

"I have to see her." Marco's voice hit her like a physical blow. "Eliza!"

She pressed her hand against the glass. Down on the street, Marco struggled against two security guards, his weathered canvas jacket a stark contrast to their pressed uniforms. His dark hair fell across his face, longer than when she'd last seen him.

"Mrs. Harrington, should we call the police?" The building manager's voice crackled through the intercom.

Eliza's throat closed. From fifteen stories up, she watched Marco break free, only to be caught again. He'd lost weight, the jacket hanging loose on his frame.

"Eliza!" His voice carried even through the thick glass. "Please explain, help me understand!"

More security personnel emerged from the building. Four men now, surrounding him. One reached for handcuffs.

"Ma'am?" The intercom crackled again.

She opened her mouth, but no sound came out. Marco's eyes swept the building's façade, searching. For a moment, just a moment, he looked directly at her window. Recognition flashed across his face.

The security team wrestled him toward a waiting car, his boots scraping against concrete. "You know the truth!" His words echoed off the surrounding buildings. "You know what really happened out there!"

A car door slammed. Engine started. The vehicle pulled away from the curb, carrying Marco into the maze of Manhattan traffic. Within seconds, it vanished around a corner.

The intercom buzzed one final time. "Mrs. Harrington? Everything's been handled. We'll increase security to prevent further incidents."

Eliza's reflection stared back at her from the window - perfect hair, perfect makeup, perfect lie. Her hand slid from the glass, leaving no trace she'd ever touched it.

Later that night, Richard's fingers dug into Eliza's waist as he guided her toward their bedroom. His breath reeked of scotch, hot against her neck.

"My trophy wife." He fumbled with her zipper. "Show everyone what they can't have."

The silk dress pooled at her feet. Richard's hands roamed possessively, marking territory. Each touch felt like sandpaper against her skin.

"The press loves us." He pushed her onto the Egyptian cotton sheets. "Such a perfect couple."

Eliza fixed her gaze on the ceiling, mind drifting to a different night, different hands. Gentle fingers tracing constellations on her skin. Whispered stories of far-off places. The way Marco's eyes had held hers in firelight, seeing her - really seeing her.

Richard grunted above her, taking what he wanted. His wedding ring caught the light, cold metal against her flesh. She performed her part, made the right sounds, moved the right way. A well-rehearsed dance, empty of meaning.

"Mine," Richard growled. The word echoed in the vast bedroom, bouncing off marble and glass.

When he finished, he rolled away, snoring within minutes. Eliza slipped into the master bathroom, locking the door with trembling fingers. The shower's spray couldn't wash away the feeling of wrongness that clung to her skin.

Steam fogged the mirrors as she sank to the heated floor. Her reflection fractured through tears - the perfect wife dissolving into something raw and real. The marble felt cold against her back, so different from rough bark, from calloused hands steadying her over uneven ground.

She pressed her fist against her mouth, muffling the sob that threatened to escape. The price of security stretched before her - endless nights like this one, trading genuine connection for gilded chains. Her other hand clutched her chest, trying to hold together something already broken.

Water ran down her face, mixing with silent tears. In the distance, city sounds filtered through thick walls - a world of luxury and emptiness, bought with a piece of her soul.

CHAPTER TWENTY-TWO

Adjustment Struggles

Eliza stared at her walk-in closet, rows of designer dresses blurring before her eyes. The silk felt wrong against her fingers, too smooth after weeks of cotton and canvas. Her calluses, earned from countless hours of gathering firewood and weaving palm fronds, caught on the delicate fabric. She pulled out a $3000 Valentino, remembering how simple it had been to choose what to wear when she only had one outfit, sun-bleached and patched with whatever they could salvage.

"The board meeting starts in an hour." Richard adjusted his tie in the mirror, shoulders squared with newfound authority. His perfectly pressed suit was a far cry from the torn shirt he'd worn for weeks. "I told them how I took charge on that island, kept everyone's spirits up."

Her hand clenched around the dress hanger until her knuckles whitened. She'd watched him huddle in the shelter's corner, complaining about the heat while Marco and she collected water, their backs burning under the merciless sun.

"Jenkins was impressed by my survival instincts." Richard's cologne filled the room, an artificial cloud suffocating after months of sea air and wood smoke. He preened, adjusting his gold cufflinks. "Said it shows real leadership potential."

Eliza's thoughts drifted to morning swims in the lagoon, fish darting between her feet like living ribbons of silver. No makeup, no pretense, no carefully curated image to maintain. Just salt water and sunshine on her skin, and the honest reflection of herself in the crystalline waters.

"We should host a dinner party." Richard gripped her shoulders from behind, his manicured nails digging into her flesh through the silk robe. "Show everyone we're back, stronger than ever. The Carmichaels and Petersons are dying to hear our story."

But they weren't stronger. The gap between them had widened into an ocean deeper than the one that had marooned them. Every practiced smile, every polite touch highlighted what they'd lost - or perhaps what had never existed beneath their carefully constructed facade.

"I thought we could take the yacht out next month." He smoothed his jacket, straightening an invisible wrinkle, missing how she flinched at the word 'yacht.' His eyes gleamed with artificial confidence. "Show everyone we're not afraid. Maybe invite the club members."

The bedroom's climate control hummed, maintaining perfect temperature with mechanical precision. Eliza longed for ocean breezes, for the honest sweat of work under the sun, for the satisfaction of earning each meal. For conversations that meant something, not this hollow performance of marriage that echoed through their marble halls.

"You seem different since we got back." Richard frowned at her reflection, his forehead creasing with genuine confusion. "More... distant. The island's over, darling. Time to be yourself again." His hand patted her shoulder with detached affection.

But that was the problem. She'd finally found herself on that beach, stripped of pretense and privilege, only to lose it in this maze of luxury and lies. The woman who had learned to spear fish and climb coconut trees was drowning in designer silk and social obligations.

CHAPTER TWENTY-THREE

One Year Anniversary

Crystal chandeliers cast prismatic light across the Grand Ballroom of the Rosewood Hotel. Eliza's Marchesa gown sparkled with each measured step, her practiced smile reflecting in the mirrored walls like a thousand perfect masks. The "Survival and Revival Gala," they'd called it - turning six months of desperate survival into an excuse for champagne and tax write-offs.

"And there she was, my brave wife, helping keep our spirits up." Richard's voice carried across the circle of rapt socialites, his hand possessive on the small of her back. "Such strength of character."

Eliza's fingers tightened around her champagne flute. The calluses had faded, leaving behind soft palms that had forgotten the grip of fishing spears and rough rope.

"Tell them about the coconuts, darling." Richard squeezed her waist, prompting her like a trained performer. "How you helped gather them."

She hadn't helped. She'd done it alone while he complained about the heat. Marco had taught her the technique before...

"Oh, it was nothing." The words fell from her lips like perfectly polished pearls. "Richard was our rock through it all."

The society wives leaned in, designer perfume mixing with expensive wine. Their eyes gleamed with the vicarious thrill of danger safely contained in anecdotes.

"You must have been terrified." Mrs. Vasquez pressed a manicured hand to her throat, diamonds catching the light. "How did you manage without proper skincare?"

Eliza's laugh tinkled like wind chimes, hollow and artificial. "You learn what really matters out there."

But what really mattered had been stripped away, replaced by this performance of gratitude and resilience. Her reflection in the ballroom windows showed a perfect society wife - coiffed, polished, empty. The woman who had found freedom in simplicity was buried beneath layers of Chanel and social obligation.

"To survival!" Richard raised his glass, basking in the attention. The crowd echoed his toast, celebrating a story they'd never understand.

Behind her smile, Eliza's eyes remained fixed on some distant point, seeing not the glittering ballroom but a simple beach where she'd once been real.

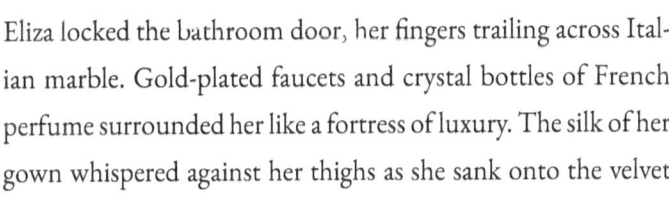

Eliza locked the bathroom door, her fingers trailing across Italian marble. Gold-plated faucets and crystal bottles of French perfume surrounded her like a fortress of luxury. The silk of her gown whispered against her thighs as she sank onto the velvet bench before the vanity.

Her reflection stared back - perfect makeup, styled hair, manicured nails. A living doll. She pressed her palm against the cool mirror, remembering calloused hands and sun-bronzed skin. The woman who had climbed palm trees and speared fish had vanished beneath layers of artificial perfection.

The memory hit like a physical blow - Marco's rough hands sliding down her bare arms as he taught her to weave palm fronds. His breath warm against her neck, voice low and rich with promise. The way their laughter echoed across empty beaches, real and unrestrained. His eyes had seen her - truly seen her - not as an accessory but as a force of nature.

Last night, Richard had touched her with entitled familiarity, his movements mechanical and predictable. She'd performed her role with practiced precision, making the right sounds at the right moments. Afterward, he'd rolled away to check his phone, already planning how to leverage their survival story at the next board meeting.

"My brave wife," he called her at parties, displaying her like a trophy. "Such composure under pressure." Each word tightened the gilded chains of expectation around her throat.

A tear slipped down her cheek, carving through expensive foundation. She'd chosen this - safety, society, status. Traded salt air and starlight for climate-controlled perfection. Sacrificed raw passion for polite affection.

The diamond on her finger caught the light, throwing fractured rainbows across the wall. Its weight dragged at her hand like an anchor, holding her in place while her true self drifted further away with each passing day.

Her shoulders shook with silent sobs as the truth crystallized - she'd survived the shipwreck only to drown in luxury, choosing slow suffocation over the terrifying freedom of real love.

Chapter Twenty-Four

News of Marco

The glossy magazine slipped from the stack of mail, land-ing open on her desk. Eliza's breath caught. There he was - Marco - standing tall against a backdrop of snow-capped mountain peaks, teaching a group of eager adventurers in ex-pensive outdoor gear how to start a fire with primitive tools.

"Wilderness Mastery: The Ultimate Survival Experience," the headline proclaimed in bold serif font. Her fingers slowly traced his image, lingering on the familiar curve of his jaw. The boyish warmth that had once made her heart flutter had vanished from his face, replaced by something harder, more guarded. His eyes, once dancing with possibility and adventure, now held the dis-tance of mountain ranges and untold stories.

The article detailed his thriving business leading wealthy clients through controlled brushes with nature, complete with gourmet camp meals and emergency satellite phones. Teaching them what she had learned beside him on that beach - but without the raw authenticity of true survival, the genuine fear and triumph that had bound them together.

More photos spread across the glossy pages, each one a fresh wound. Marco demonstrating shelter building, his muscled arms lifting pine branches into perfect A-frames. Teaching navigation under star-filled skies that mirrored nights they'd spent tracking constellations together, huddled close against the ocean breeze. But his smile never reached his eyes anymore, as if some vital spark had been extinguished.

Salt water splashed onto the glossy paper, blurring the professionally staged images. Not ocean spray this time - her own tears marking what could have been. Every laugh they'd shared over makeshift meals, every charged moment of connection in the wilderness, every future they might have built together - all sacrificed for the safety of her gilded cage and family expectations.

"Still obsessing over the hired help?" Richard's voice cut through her reverie, sharp as a blade. He stood in the doorway, straightening his silk tie with manicured fingers that had never known real work or the satisfaction of survival.

"Just an interesting article about survival training." Her voice emerged steady, practiced from years of concealing her true feelings. The smile slid into place like a well-worn mask as she closed the magazine with deliberate casualness.

"Darling, we've moved beyond all that unpleasantness." He waved his hand dismissively, his platinum wedding band catching the light. "The charity gala committee is waiting, and you know how Miranda gets when we're late."

Eliza rose, smoothing her designer dress against her thighs. The woman who had once found freedom in Marco's arms was sealed away now, preserved like a pressed flower between the pages of society's expectations - beautiful, perfect, and dead. Their paths had split on that rescue beach, dividing like rivers that would never meet again, one flowing toward wilderness and authenticity, the other toward marble halls and hollow smiles.

She followed Richard from the room, her heels clicking on hardwood, leaving the magazine - and her true self - behind in the growing shadows.

CHAPTER TWENTY-FIVE

Back to the Norm

Richard's hands, confident and demanding, slid around Eliza's waist, pulling her close. "You've been distant lately," he murmured, his breath hot on her neck. "Time to remind you what you're here for."

Eliza let him guide her towards the bed, her body moving on autopilot, a marionette obeying its strings. Her mind was elsewhere, drifting on ocean currents, tracing constellations with calloused fingers under a vast night sky.

She knelt before him, her hands mechanically unfastening his belt. The silk of his pants whispered against her skin, a hollow echo of the rough fabric of Marco's cargo shorts brushing against her leg as they'd huddled together for warmth.

Tears pricked at the corners of her eyes, silent sentinels of her true feelings. She blinked them back, leaning forward to fulfill her wifely duties. Richard's hands fisted in her hair, control-ling, possessive. His groans filled the room, a stark contrast to Marco's tender whispers, the soft hum of appreciation he'd emit when she'd simply lean into his touch.

Flashes of memory flickered behind her closed lids. Marco's rough thumb brushing away a tear, his warm breath mingling with hers as they shared a tentative first kiss. The way his eyes, soft and tender, would trace her face as if she were the most precious thing he'd ever seen. The warmth of his embrace, a sanctuary found amidst the harsh reality of their survival.

Richard shuddered, satisfaction evident in his sharp exhale. He released her, stepping back to fasten his pants, a smug smile playing on his lips. Eliza rose, wiping her mouth with the back of her hand, the taste of him bitter on her tongue.

She turned away, her reflection in the mirror catching her eye. The woman staring back at her was a stranger, hollow-eyed and empty. She'd traded her soul for silk sheets and diamonds, her body a currency to maintain her gilded cage. The true cost of her transaction was laid bare in the stark emptiness of her gaze. Physical intimacy without emotional connection left her with nothing but a void, a chasm where her heart used to be.

———◆◇◆———

Eliza stepped onto the penthouse balcony, the city lights below a poor substitute for the stars that had guided them on the island.

Her manicured fingers traced the cold glass railing, so different from the rough bark of the shelter she'd built with Marco.

The night air carried a chill, but she didn't move. The discomfort felt right, felt real - unlike the temperature-controlled perfection of her gilded cage. A shooting star streaked across the sky, and her chest tightened. She remembered lying on the beach, Marco's arm around her as he taught her the constellations, his voice soft and sure, his calloused fingers pointing out Orion's Belt against the velvet darkness.

Her reflection in the glass showed a perfect society wife - expertly styled hair, designer dress, flawless makeup. But beneath that carefully constructed façade, cracks spread like spider webs through her soul. The mask she wore grew heavier with each passing day, threatening to shatter under its own weight.

A sob caught in her throat, raw and unexpected. Her hand flew to her mouth, perfectly painted nails digging into her skin. For just a moment, the carefully maintained walls crumbled, and real tears carved paths through her expensive foundation, leaving trails of vulnerability she couldn't hide.

The diamond on her finger caught the city lights, throwing rainbow prisms across her face. She'd chosen this - wealth, status, security. Traded sand between her toes for marble floors, fresh-caught fish for caviar, true connection for hollow small talk at charity galas where everyone wore masks as thick as her own.

On the island, she'd discovered who she really was - strong, capable, alive. With Marco, she'd found a love that saw past her polished exterior to the woman beneath. He'd shown her a different kind of life, one measured in sunrises and shared laughter rather than social obligations and bank accounts. His hands had been rough but gentle, his heart pure and uncomplicated by society's expectations.

But she'd walked away. Chosen the path she'd been groomed for since childhood. Now that door was closed forever, locked and sealed by her own hand. The woman who'd found freedom on that beach was gone, replaced by this perfect automaton in Chanel, who smiled on command and never let the world see her break. Each breath in this rarefied air was another small death of the person she could have been.

Eliza slipped off her Louboutins, the red soles a mockery of the blood pumping through her veins. The cool concrete of the balcony pressed against her bare feet, grounding her in this moment of crystal clarity. The night air carried the scent of expensive perfume and broken promises.

Her fingers traced the smooth metal railing as memories flooded her mind. Marco's face when she'd told him her decision haunted her - the way his eyes had dimmed, like stars fading at dawn. He hadn't begged or pleaded. His quiet dignity had made it worse. The salt-laden breeze of that final day still stung her nostrils.

"I need to think of my future," she'd said, the words tasting like ash in her mouth. Each syllable had felt like swallowing broken glass.

"Your future, or your fear?" His voice had been soft, under-standing even in his pain. The gentleness of his accusation had cut deeper than anger ever could.

The city lights blurred through her tears as she climbed onto the railing. Forty stories up, the wind whipped her hair free from its perfect coif. For the first time since leaving the island, she felt something close to the freedom she'd known there. The city stretched endlessly below, a glittering maze of artificial stars.

She remembered Marco's hands, strong and sure, teaching her to weave palm fronds for their shelter. The way he'd looked at her like she was precious, not just pretty. The sound of his laugh, real and deep, so different from Richard's calculated chuckles at charity events. Those memories burned brighter than any diamond Richard had ever given her.

Her designer dress caught on the railing as she steadied her-self. One small step separated her from release. From escape. From the end of this hollow existence she'd chosen. The silk whispered against metal, a final farewell to luxury.

The shame of her choice pressed down on her chest, heavier than all of Richard's gifts combined. She'd traded real love for a facade, freedom for a cage of her own making. Each breath felt like drowning in champagne.

Eliza took that final step forward, and in that moment, all her pain, all her regrets, simply ceased to exist. The night swallowed her whole, a dark mercy she hadn't deserved but claimed any-way.

Afterword

Dear Readers,

Thank you so much for embarking on this journey with me through "Savage Tides." Your support means the world to me, and I appreciate you taking the time to immerse yourself in Eliza's story.

I have to tell you, in the original ending to Eliza's tale, I had envisioned her crying on the balcony, contemplating her decision as she overlooked the city and then basically fading to black. However, I felt it needed to resonate more deeply, and the ending evolved into something that ultimately affected me on a personal level. It was a hard choice to let Eliza go, as I found myself falling in love with her character. I couldn't shake the grief of her loss, nor could I ignore the profound impact her choices had on the lives around her—Marco, Richard, and of course, herself.

While the ending may be darker than some might expect, it was important to me that it authentically reflected the depth of her feelings and the consequences of her decisions. I hope that you found the intensity of her emotions as moving as I did while writing. It is so hard letting a character go. I will admit I wrestled with the ending. I also shed some tears when I finally wrote the ending. I couldn't help but think of the devastation her choices made in the lives of everyone around her.

On a different note, I want to share that "Savage Tides" marks my first step into the realm of traditional romance. If you've enjoyed this book, I invite you to explore the other titles I have written, which you can find in the "Also By" section that follows. A word of warning, these works delve into a more graphic erotica genre, capturing a different kind of passion. The experience of writing "Savage Tides" has inspired me to pursue more ideas in line with more romance, and I'm excited to share these with you in the future.

If you found joy in this book, please consider leaving a review—it truly helps me and my work reach more readers. Also, for the latest news and updates on upcoming releases, please visit my website at JulieFreebush.com.

Thank you once again for your support and for allowing me to share this piece of my heart with you.

With love and gratitude,

Julie Freebush

About Julie Freebush

Passionate and Dedicated

Ever wondered what it's like to live a life filled with passion, desire, and forbidden love?

Meet Julie Freebush, the author who knows no bounds when it comes to exploring the realms of *eroticism*.

Julie has had an intense fascination with *seduction* and *temptation* since her childhood, when an innocent skinny dipping experience sparked something deep inside her.

Her stories are filled with *seduction*, *temptation*, and *illicit encounters* that will leave you *breathless*.

Julie spends her days *writing* and her nights "*Researching*".

As an author who knows no bounds.

Julie's experiences range from the ***scandalous*** to the downright ***explicit***, and her writing is a testament to her ***insatiable appetite for pleasure***.

Julie's works are filled with ***secrets, lust, and explicit encounters*** that will leave your heart racing. So, if you're ready to embark on a journey of ***sensuality*** and ***illicit pleasure***, join ***Julie Freebush*** in her world of ***Short & Steamy Tales of Erotica***.

For all the latest releases and current happenings with Julie, stop by her website. JulieFreeb ush.com

Also by Julie Freebush

Savage Tides: Survival and Desire

Julie's Unabridged ADULT Research Stories Series

Short and Steamy Tales of Erotica:

Volumes One & Two

Home From the Army: Book One An Erotic Tale of Passion, Seduction, Family and Forbidden Desires